PENGUIN BOOKS

SITA'S ASCENT

Dr Vayu Naidu brought her research and performance of oral traditions into the British academy, and created new works with composers and orchestras and for theatre and radio drama. This is her debut novel. The Vayu Naidu Storytelling Company is based in London.

SITA'S
ASCENT

VAYU NAIDU

PENGUIN BOOKS

An imprint of Penguin Random House

PENGUIN BOOKS

USA | Canada | UK | Ireland | Australia
New Zealand | India | South Africa | China | Singapore

Penguin Books is part of the Penguin Random House group of companies
whose addresses can be found at global.penguinrandomhouse.com

Published by Penguin Random House India Pvt. Ltd
4th Floor, Capital Tower 1, MG Road,
Gurugram 122 002, Haryana, India

First published by Penguin Books India 2012

10 9 8 7 6 5 4 3 2

ISBN 9780143415282

Typeset in Plantin by InoSoft Systems, Noida
Printed at Repro India Limited

www.penguin.co.in

MIX
Paper from
responsible sources
FSC® C047271

This is a legitimate digitally printed version of the book and therefore might not
have certain extra finishing on the cover.

For Chris Banfield and Lakshmi Holmström and
my father, Major General Aban Naidu, who revealed the
epic in life

Contents

Ramayana

Rama is to be crowned King of Ayodhya. His wife is to be the queen. The coronation is interrupted. His father's favourite wife, Queen Kaikeyi, exiles Rama to the forests for fourteen years where he must roam unrecognizable as a royal. Sita is determined to accompany him and Rama's brother Lakshmana will not be left behind. During their time in the forests they encounter sages, rakshasas, ferrymen, tribals, hunters, spirits and the common folk.

In the thirteenth year of exile Sita is enchanted by a golden deer and pleads with Rama to catch it so she can return to Ayodhya after the exile with the creature as a reminder of their time in the forests. When Rama leaves, only because he sees Sita distressed on losing sight of the deer, Sita hears Rama's voice crying for help. Lakshmana is unable to convince her that it is a rakshasa's trick. She hurls at him a fatal remark that makes Lakshmana depart hastily in search of Rama. Left unguarded, except by a protective line drawn on the earth by Lakshmana, Sita is abducted by the machinations of the emperor Ravana and held captive in his kingdom.

The search for Sita on the princes' return to their forest dwelling begins with their meeting Hanuman, the chief minister to the exiled King Sugriva. Hanuman, with his special powers and wisdom, is able to find Sita. When she tells him of her trials he urges her to return with him. But she does not wish to return by stealth; she feels a world order needs to be changed from might to right, from darkness to light.

A war is waged, and Ravana is killed by Rama. When Sita appears before Rama after the great war, he informs her in public hearing that she is free from captivity. Sita is incensed that she should have to prove her 'purity' so she orders Lakshmana to light a fire. As she walks through the fire, that is, undergoes an agnipariksha, Agni, the god of fire, appeals to Rama about Sita's unparalleled and uncorrupted love for her husband.

Fourteen years have passed and Sita and Rama, with Lakshmana and Hanuman, return to Ayodhya. Rama is crowned king. Sita is expecting their child and our story begins from here.

Sita

When the shock subsided she could hear again. The sound of the wheels grinding recklessly on the stony track faded into the distance. Her grip on her left hand tightened. Her bangle twisted and snapped. She gasped to discover her feet rooted to the spot while her heart pounded, making her body twitch. White lips, dry mouth, white light. Like a primeval beginning, there was a sound and a string of images in her head, without meaning. Where words once flowed with lightness from the heart, there was now a forest fire. 'When . . . did all this happen?' she asked herself.

They had been driving in the chariot for at least two hours. The paved roads gave way to rougher bypasses and then

1

slip roads west of the capital to tracks in the forest. The breeze from the speed of the open vehicle tousled her hair. She didn't care. She was so happy recounting: 'That first time Urmilla and I walked through here, we heard the drums at the palace announcing our arrival. Do you remember?'

No response from the driver. He cracked the whip and the horses charged like lightning. Parrots flew past, shrieking in their rice-field-green plumage lined with pomegranate pink. 'Our hearts were beating fast as the dancers seemed to leap down from the trees to welcome us. As young brides, we thought this was the gateway to the world of our husbands!' The same happiness flooded her now, so she could override his silence. Her hand cupped her pregnant belly; she was six months past. 'When we took our vows we circled Agni seven times, and,' she continued, half laughing to herself, 'over the years, we've all travelled seven worlds of wonder, joy, fear, anger, even courage, with fire . . . wouldn't you say, Lakshmana?' Sita looked at him, and he steadily faced the path ahead of him, looking above the white rumps of the speeding horses and their red reins as the chariot drove on.

'I sent a message to Valmiki,' was Lakshmana's reply. Teasingly she said, 'I hope you didn't give too much away. I want to test his memory!' Lakshmana smiled in spite of himself. Yes, she was referring to the great storyteller who chronicled events of mythological proportions. He remembered beyond memory, and now Sita was going to playfully challenge him. Lakshmana slowed the chariot down, as this part of the forest had low-lying boughs and the pathway meandered into shrubs. The hermitage also had protected deer roaming nearby. The dwellings were camouflaged. This encouraged deer, peacocks and wild cats to come and feed there, trusting the few male and female ascetics who lived in the huts.

Lakshmana brought the chariot to a halt a few yards from the clearing where the huts stood. Each hut sloped or stood straight depending on the length of the branches that had been cut to build it. Crowned with a thatch of dried leaves, each hut was lined with mud. The aroma of the sap from the freshly cut branches hung in the midday air. Lakshmana and Sita took a deep breath. Smell: the essence of memory. The smell of the past with associations recalling personal worlds. This smell evoked a memory of comfort. Even Lakshmana relaxed his tense muscles as he removed the harness from the horses and gave them water. 'I am here, and this is now,' he told himself. Swiftly, he went to Sita's side as she held her belly and stepped out of the chariot. 'Amma,' she uttered with relief as her feet touched the ground. He watched as she took in her surroundings. Then she began to hand him the various earthen vessels covered with plantain leaves containing gifts for Valmiki and fellow ascetics. First were the gifts of food. She steadied herself and pulled the sari pallu over her shoulder as she walked towards the clearing with one ceremonial vessel for Valmiki. Lakshmana, cradling the other vessels in his arms, followed her.

'Aaaarrh!' came a squealing grunt of welcome from Valmiki as he emerged from his hut. He stretched his arms and interlocked his palms skyward to make a stupa over his head. He did not look much like a wise, aging sage. His creativity swirled all around him, in little atoms of cheer. His upper body was bare with matted hair covering his back and chest. His quick, shuffling stride revealed he was simultaneously embarrassed and proud of his sizeable belly. Valmiki smelt of wood smoke, bark and ghee. These were the auspicious ingredients for sacred fires, around which he often sat, chuckling merrily as he taught, or gazing silently as he composed. His laughter, which was a cross between a donkey braying and a heralding trumpet, resounded through the forest. The birds of the forest fluttered down to complete the reception for Sita, who was paying a visit nearly two years after returning to Ayodhya and the coronation.

Valmiki approached her with his broken-toothed smile. 'How long has it been, Sita?'

'Too long, Maharaj,' Sita said as she started to bend to touch his feet. He had earned the appellation 'Maharaj' as he was celebrated as the king of all known and unknown storytellers. 'Now, now, none of that,' said Valmiki. 'It is awkward for you, not only because you are a queen but because you have a belly too!' He cackled. Lakshmana shook with laughter as he set the vessels down and seamlessly stretched himself on the ground to touch the old sage's feet and seek his blessings. Sita knelt. 'And Rama?' Valmiki inquired.

'Rama sends you his deepest love, Maharaj. He knew I wanted to monopolize this time with you!' Sita said, her eyes shining.

'It is a time of transition, Maharaj . . . too many demands on his time. Bharata's administration is flawless. It is the ruling on domestic statutes that's pressing and Rama wanted to attend to them personally,' Lakshmana offered.

Valmiki caught the hint of an apology and responded with the deftness of a diplomat. 'Fourteen years is a long time to be away . . . not to say you all haven't been busy; but it's that shift from the individual to the state—every decision is slower because you have to take a whole lot of people into consideration, isn't it?'

Valmiki could sense Lakshmana's unease. Lakshmana knew of his ruler's difficult position, where taking decisions meant consultation with ministers, which at the best of times was time-consuming, and at worst, unwieldy in matters of urgency.

Valmiki cheerfully beckoned one of the ascetics who served Sita a leaf cup of goat's milk mixed with honey. Smell and taste: they immediately conjured up days in the forest and hospitality at hermitages. Sita couldn't help herself and said, 'I've added to this recipe, you know. A dust of cardamom with some crushed pistachio makes it a royal drink for regal hermits!' Valmiki understood her well and burst into his high-pitched laughter. 'Pista, ah yes. Now that is something I would have to spend a lot of time shelling. I don't have the patience of Sabari.'

'Is that why you wrote her in?' asked Lakshmana cautiously. Valmiki's gaze steadied beyond Lakshmana's face. 'She was real. How else can anyone comprehend that degree of devotion?'

'Did it not contradict our entire system about maintaining purity when you made her taste every single fruit she offered Rama?'

'But it's her love, Lakshmana, which went beyond all that,' said Sita. 'You see, I wouldn't think twice about what I cooked and fed my friends—only because I would be making it with love.' How could anyone argue with that. The banter continued and gradually the other ascetics joined them, giving news about how the forest spring had widened and changed its course.

After lunch Valmiki insisted Sita have the customary nap inside the hut. Lakshmana unloaded Sita's luggage. Since returning to the palace the same day was impossible, it had been decided that Lakshmana would return to escort her home. Rama was particular about these arrangements. Sita had instructed her maids on cooking and cleaning the inner apartments for the few days until her return. Coming to the forest to spend time with Valmiki was almost like going to her mother's home. Sita's mother had died a few years ago when she got news that her daughter had been abducted by a shape-shifting king and was being held hostage in Lanka. The thought of contamination by strangers' touch and her daughter's life in danger made her wither into a skeleton. Her last words were: 'What will people say?'

Sita's mind began to wander as she came out of a restful doze, woken by the murmur of distant bees. The afternoon sun filtered through the slatted window as the trees cast long shadows across the clearing. Sita sat up. Valmiki stood with his hands on his hips, watching Lakshmana pile wood to start the fire for cooking the evening meal. Sita was offered hot tea made with ginger, cloves and cinnamon. It got her circulation going. Lakshmana tied a knot with dried blades of grass and set the wood down. Picking two flints, he struck them decisively. He set the spark near the knot of grass and blew on it. 'Not too big a flame, Lakshmana!' cautioned Valmiki. Lakshmana's face reddened with pain and rage. 'Too much water under the bridge,' thought Sita as she saw him wince.

She knew what Lakshmana was thinking. It wasn't that long ago when everyone had stood around—the victorious and the defeated. Nothing had been conquered. Sita was called to prove that she was worthy of all the lives that had been lost in the war at Lanka. Is she 'pure', they wanted to know. 'After all, her captor and host Ravana was deeply and madly in love with her,' whispered the columns of soldiers who had survived the war. Sita stood beleaguered watching the scene unfold before her eyes. She had been in captivity for thirteen months with no human contact. Her desolation vanished in an instant, a wave of relief surging over her, when she saw Rama tending to a wounded soldier. And when Rama looked up, the flame in her glowed with joy. It was him. He, who had vanquished the darkness that was eroding the world. He was the one for whom she had waited and waited.

Rama stood before the columns of the depleted army and their malicious murmurs, and the words he uttered she first heard in slow motion. When she could made sense of them, everything dissolved into disbelief. The flame within her burst into a rage. Somewhere deep inside she knew that all of those who stood there, grieving the loss of their dear ones, wanted in exchange for the cost of flesh something invaluable—moral fibre. If the dead could not return, then those left behind wanted purity as the price of blood. Rama said to Sita, 'Ravana is dead. You are free to go now.' Was it Rama speaking or their spokesman? 'Light a fire, Lakshmana!' she commanded. 'Let the flame burn brighter!' she hissed. Lakshmana was stunned. Her eyes were ablaze, her voice was fire as he struck the flint and it sparked. In the here and now of this hermitage, Sita could see Lakshmana had not forgotten that moment, and she comforted him in her thoughts: 'It will all come to pass. We live in a different time now.'

Lakshmana neatly stacked in Sita's dwelling the supply of vegetables, rice, grain, utensils and palm leaves for writing—gifts for everyone at the hermitage. Next to these was a modest trunk with Sita's clothes. Sita made a mental inventory of all the things that had to be unloaded from the chariot as she had instructed their packing. Lakshmana headed towards the horses and harnessed them. They were calm and ready to be driven. Valmiki followed Sita as she bade Lakshmana goodbye: 'Please tell Rama not to work too late. See that he drinks enough watermelon juice during the day; the circles under his eyes have grown very dark. Oh! Tell Urmilla everything is just as I expected it to be here, in fact, even better. Next time she must come too. Go carefully, Lakshmana, and I'll see you on Dasami. I'll be waiting.'

'No, Sita,' was what she first heard him say. This time he looked straight at her, as if to bridle the pain he was wrestling with as he said these words. 'Rama . . . instructed me . . . I am to leave you here. You are not to return. Those were Rama's words.'

The shock of the sound of his voice, the look in his eyes. It was a primeval beginning. White light, dry mouth, white lips. A string of images floated in white clouds behind her eyes; they were bereft of all meaning. Her left hand rose to hold her throat. Her right hand clasped its wrist. Her bangle snapped. The figure floating away in the chariot was a man called Lakshmana. She repeated the name in her mind: *Lakshmana*. The more she did the more he evaporated from her memory. It, he, had no meaning. The sound filtered in and she could hear the wheels of the chariot grinding recklessly on the pathway in the distance. The clouds of dust they raised made Valmiki sneeze. Sita let out the first scream. A short one and held her belly tight.

Words, which came so easily to Valmiki, now burned on his tongue. What do you say to a woman who has been abandoned, and that too, so many times?

'When?' she uttered. She felt cold and shivered in the afternoon heat. In the distance there was a sound like crashing. She was tumbling down in a spiral within herself the way Lakshmana's chariot was tumbling down the gorge. He was flying through the air, kicking his legs for the last time.

'When . . . did all this happen?' she asked. 'Why didn't he tell me?' A soft bulb of white light burst in her mind's eye. Rama was standing as she was ready to step into the chariot. He looked at her and her heart melted. He even said he was going to miss her. How long ago was this planned? She was tumbling fast and Valmiki wanted to catch her before she fell into that dark abyss of betrayal.

'This is good,' he said. 'Sita, I was born from the darkness. Listen,' said Valmiki with urgency and music in his voice. She lifted her head; somewhere inside her there was a doll called Sita, tumbling.

'Listen. When that strange man came, the one they called Narada, I thought he was another joke. I threatened him and he presented me with a challenge: "Go and see if anyone in your family will visit death in your stead and take your sins on their heads." I was so sure everyone would. My father was having his afternoon smoke and, when I asked him, he accused me of wanting to kill him. My beloved mother said I was a snake, and my darling wife accused me of attempting the greatest murder because I was wiping the smile off her face by asking her to visit death and take my sins upon her head. Till then I had been so sure they all loved me. I risked my life every day for them, I thought. I thought they loved me for me. But I did not know that I only loved myself and, naturally, they, themselves; and whom I killed, what I brought home or how I risked my life was really of no concern to anyone. My home suddenly struck me as a wilderness. I ran for my life. I returned to untie that strange man. He could see what had transpired from the way I looked. He gave me a word. I repeated it for what seemed like years on end and, out of that darkness, worlds began to swim out of my heart and sing inside my head. I could see the future and Rama, and you.'

'Did you see me like this?' Sita asked him. Valmiki hung his head. Had he imagined her as a character for the compelling epic as he saw her now? Was she to always stand tall and take the blows her husband's fate dealt her? Had he never seen her as a victim? That for a long time to come she would have to be the ideal by whom women swore when they took their marriage vows? He suddenly realized what a burden this must be.

He had so far chronicled events; he now had to tell the history of the heart. Sita exiled by Rama was a cold fact. This was not just Sita. This was Sita with child who faced him. Her eyes looked into the distance. She stood there, a woman abandoned. Holding her belly with both hands she said, 'How will my child bear his name?'

Valmiki had to learn to listen to her story from a primeval beginning, the way consciousness enters a foetus still forming.

Urmilla

In the palace, night came with the swiftness of a traveller's tiredness. It was a windless day even by the river Sarayu, and everyone welcomed an early night in Ayodhya. On still days, the night blossoms, exuding their opiate perfumes, sat snug in the gardens. Unwavering flames of oil lamps stood like sentinels guarding the centre of the courtyard of each home. Mosquitoes whimpered past. Children clung to their mothers, sleeping heavily, while men and women caressed their dreams as if these were predictions worth investing in.

Rama worked till late, examining land taxes and deeds, and he too rubbed his eyes wearily trying to forget the weight of the day. His head drooped like a ripe coconut from a palm tree and sleep dulled all his senses as he slumped over the scrolls of the maps of his kingdom. Urmilla was the last to snuff out the oil lamp in her apartments. She bathed her arms in the moonlight, wondering how Sita would be sleeping in the hermitage, wondering if there would be crickets there too, conversing so late into the night.

Even after all these years, when the sisters-in-law met, they entered the inner courtyard of girlhood familiarity. Over the last few months, now that Sita was pregnant, Urmilla had created a checklist of her cravings. They seemed different from most pregnant women in Ayodhya. 'Your child bears the mark of a foreigner,' Urmilla said the other day as she came in hastily with a bowl of soft skinned almonds. Sita loosened her hair for the massage before her bath. Both women looked at each other. Urmilla bit her lip and said, 'Oh, Sita, I didn't mean . . .' Sita burst out laughing. 'Of course, you didn't mean what you said.' Urmilla was embarrassed. It was too clumsy a mistake and, relieved by Sita's quick response, she began to chew the soft almonds before she offered them to Sita. 'All I really wished to say was that this child will bear the mark of our birthplace, Mithila.'

Sita lay down on the mat ready for the warm oil, scented with camphor and hibiscus leaves, to be massaged into her long, bee-black hair. Urmilla's fingertips were firm, pressing all the pressure points at the back of her neck.

Sita winced with pleasure as the tension was released from her neck.

'How strangely time heals, Urmi. I had never thought I would be able to laugh so easily about the whole foreigner thing,' Sita said thoughtfully. 'Some were eager for me to return. But how quick the others were to test me and see if I had indeed given in to Ravana.'

'Be careful, Sita. After all these years, much as Ayodhya is our home now, we too are foreigners here,' Urmilla said as she looked towards the door, hoping no one was listening. Ravana was a dreaded name even after his death. 'After all, when women marry they get adopted by their husbands' people,' she continued.

'I think we need to turn that urn of thinking around, Urmi! When we left Mithila we were not orphans. Our husbands came in search of us.'

'Well, they didn't actually come *in search* of us. There was a challenge announced for your swayamvara, inviting princes from all around,' Urmilla added, smiling, mocking Sita's claims about Rama and Lakshmana making it their mission to seek brides.

'Yes, but Rama and Lakshmana happened to be there because Vishwamitra brought them after restoring peace to Dandaka forest—and who knows what plans destiny had for us all to come together in this lifetime. Anyway, the point I was making was that we women have to change things around—our husbands' homes do not adopt us; we adopt *them* and create homes and families around them.'

Urmilla kissed Sita's forehead, saying, 'Long may that thought prevail, Sita. Let your child hear that and carry it forward, whether it is a son or a daughter.' She was swift in moving from the role of friend and oracle-bearer to that of masseuse. 'Okay, now let's see how the great belly is doing.' Sita swept the cloth off her belly. The shaft of sunlight peeping through the skylight of the bath chamber swathed her belly.

Urmilla anointed her palms with warm coconut oil and placed them on the sides of Sita's stomach. 'Great mover! I hope he's a dancer first, then a warrior,' she said.

'How are you so sure it is a he?'

'Protrusion of the belly. Pushing its way into the world, only a man can do that,' Urmilla said with her arched brow and cheeky smile. They both giggled abashedly.

Sita sighed with happy exhaustion. Urmilla began to gently massage the oil on the stretched skin of the stomach and hummed softly. Sita drifted into a doze for a few seconds. The sun's rays had shifted and a delicious aroma wafted in from the royal kitchen. As she woke, Sita placed her hand on Urmilla's and said, 'You know, a foreigner is not just someone from another place. Here it has come to mean someone who is threatening because he thinks or acts differently. And, when they feel threatened by difference, they call it "evil". They have now become quick to associate Ravana with what is foreign, therefore different; and different equals evil. But difference is not evil. That's what has become the curse of us women, coming from a different place with different ways of doing things. Oh, Urmilla, let us vow that this child will never be made to feel a stranger here in Ayodhya, at Mithila, or anywhere in the world.'

Urmilla knew how the trial by fire, the agnipariksha, had made Sita burn with anger, not shame. After all, when she had been asked to prove her purity in public, Sita was the one who had called out to Agni and the essence of fire as ammunition in her defence. Only a woman who possessed such an infinite capacity to love could go through that—not for her man, or to justify herself to the world, but because she raged against the inquisition all women had to face. 'How dare anyone question me?' Sita would sometimes mutter under her breath. Urmilla initially thought this was the Sita of their youth in Mithila, positioning herself occasionally as a royal in a moment of an adolescent tantrum. But soon it was clear that Sita was reworking in her mind the ordeal she had been through when she was held hostage in Ravana's exquisite Asokavan garden. It was exquisite to the visitor, but the mental traps that were constantly being set and changed to utterly confuse everyone about what was real required the moral and physical resilience of a martial art guru. So when she was released and asked to demonstrate how 'pure' she was, everything within Sita rankled. Urmilla wondered: 'Was there ever any choice? She was lucky she fell in love with Rama. But between being married and touched by one man who was the husband and being abducted and held hostage—or, as others would say, according to convenience, being "kept"—by another, how many women could tell the difference?' It was the ritual of marriage—the vows taken for the family, the state, for the protection of the future, the children not yet born—which sanctified the relationship in everyone's eyes. Sita had reached a point past caring for social opinion. She not only knew what the truth was but wanted to stand in for every other person who was challenged about their innocence, whether it was within relationships or for the sake of social opinion. It was clear from the way Sita would look straight into anyone's eyes—Urmilla's, of the maids-in-waiting, the servants', or Rama's—when she gave an instruction or was queried. She was without artifice and challenged anyone, royal or subject, who was conciliatory towards her. In Sita, there had emerged a strange combination of being open but also on guard.

'I should have come with you into exile. I would have massaged your neck and back every night after those long treks. Then you wouldn't have had these tension knots all along the back of your neck!'

'Aha! But you can't deny that exile made my hair grow long and heavy—that's what's giving me the tension. Can you imagine, Urmi, if I had to coil all this hair on top of my head like the sages!'

'Mm, I don't think your head is hard enough for it, Sita,' Urmilla replied. They both laughed at themselves, remembering the time when they were girls in Mithila, acting in religious dance dramas depicting life-denying ascetics and seductive courtesans.

During the day Rama was busy with affairs that brought people from different parts of the kingdom to seek his audience, offer counsel or represent grievances and inform him directly. In the afternoon, before lunch he would be briefed on matters within the court and its councils. He would retreat to his palace where Sita waited for them to have lunch together, as Urmilla would hurry back to her apartments to wait for Lakshmana.

Lakshmana's hair was greying at the temples. He was less short-tempered now than when he had left for the forest. Urmilla and he had just been married at the time. He was deep in thought, oblivious to her entering the room with a pitcher of buttermilk. She touched his shoulder and he burst into a quick, reflexive smile. 'It takes time, Urmi,' he said impatiently, frustrated with himself.

She put the pitcher down and sat on the cool stone floor beside him. 'Let it take all the time, my dearest. The most important thing is that you have returned.'

He placed her hands on his face as she began to massage his throbbing temples. Urmilla held him close and whispered soothingly, 'It takes time—for thirteen years there was the forest. You haven't even completed two years since your return here. At least Rama and Sita had each other. Do you know how much I ached for you? I still cannot believe this is real—to be able to hold you like this.'

Tears streamed down Lakshmana's face. A woman's tenderness was so foreign to him. It wound itself like a sapling around his heart, bursting with buds. Lakshmana had increasingly been having headaches since returning to Ayodhya. After years in the forest and being on guard, and then the war, he could not think of anything else but Rama's safety. He no longer had a sense of himself. Adjusting to city life and a companion, Urmilla, was difficult. The long years of celibacy had created a feeling of distance. Having someone waiting for him was piecing him back together. She was a part of his being that felt necessary but foreign. Being a husband and having a wife required new codes of behaviour, almost a different language. He found it strange not to fly into a rage any more; it was uncharacteristic. Urmilla, in her wisdom, could read his troubled heart and his loyal mind. For Lakshmana, while performing his role as a beloved younger brother and as councillor in the kingdom, Rama and the state were inextricably bound together. Strangely, Urmilla could see how it held Lakshmana together, and how it also tore him apart.

When Rama entered his chambers, Sita was bustling with the aarti platter, the flame burning brightly in its centre. She waved it steadily clockwise before him, from right upper arm to above the forehead to the left shoulder and down to his knee, circling it three times and finally placing the vermilion mark on his forehead. It was a ritual to keep out sinister spirits and malevolent energies encountered during the morning duties. She looked at him through the camphor's flame. The flame was a window for both of them to focus on. She, smiling but looking at him intently; he, disturbing her steady gaze with a smile that hovered at the corner of his lips. It was his way of saying: 'After all those deep and dark forests, here we are, urbanized, wearing fancy clothes. A fine drama—these waves of life. Let's enjoy this act for now.'

That's how she greeted him home for lunch every day since they had returned. In fact, that was also how the news of her pregnancy became public, when she deftly handed the aarti platter to a maid of honour and fainted, with Rama quick to catch her fall. Today, when all the maids-in-waiting slowly bowed and left the dining hall, Sita and Rama smiled at each other. It was after a long time now that, through the scaffolds of daily rituals, they were returning to their former selves.

Exile had made them strangers to a life in court. Sometimes living in a palace struck them as yet another brief sojourn from the forest. In the late evenings they were, independently, haunted by the prospect of preparing for a departure.

Exile is not dislocation, it is a rising sense of loss. The loss of time and experience amidst the whirlpool of life. Quite simply, there was a lot to converse about, but the hopelessness of being left behind dogged them. The real challenge lay in moving forward in spite of feeling paralysed. They constantly straddled the emotional geographies of exile and royal luxury. They had begun to realize that moving across geographically, covering the terrain of forests, mountains, rivers, even an ocean, was more bearable than defining an emotional geography. With two in a companionship, how did one map what was unseen in the other? Even in oneself? At last, a bridge had emerged between them—Rama and Sita's child, yet to be born. This foetus was the desire for life swimming in a limitless ocean within the universe of the womb. It sparked a new channel of communication between them.

Sita led Rama to his place. The banana leaf had been spread on the gold platter. The first morsel of lentils and rice drizzled with pure ghee was offered to the gods. The crows across the courtyard cawed with delight, acknowledging that they, who were visiting as the spirits of the ancestors, had been fed, and now the living could continue with their meal. The temple bells began their orbit of sound. Rama sat and as Sita served him the curried yam and plantain, she said, 'The salt seller came by today. She told me a fine story.'

'Let me guess,' said Rama as he dipped his finger in the yam sauce and licked it. 'Was it about how one day people will have to pay for salt?'

'You don't say! Are we coming to that? Cheh! What a day that will be when we have to pay for what's in our blood! No, no, thank god it was nothing like that. It was about a woman who had been blessed by Surya and had a vision that she must tell the story to everyone.'

'Why? Didn't she want to keep that vision to herself?'

'Naturally, possessing a woman's generosity, she wanted to share it with everyone.'

'Did anyone listen?' Rama asked as he drew the rice to the centre of the leaf plate awaiting the next course.

Sita now served him spinach. Pouring tamarind soup on his rice she said, 'Of course not. Finally, she found a pregnant salt seller who said she would listen, but fell off to sleep.'

'This is getting increasingly believable,' said Rama as he reached out for a poppadom and cracked it.

'But then a voice from within the womb said, "I will listen." So the old woman sang a song:

'Listen to this song, and its good luck will follow you—

You will turn ruined ghost towns into bustling cities;

Where there are dry cotton fields you will fill its branches with pearls,

You will return lost treasures buried under the sea to the shore

And you will even bring the dead back to life.'

'What an extraordinary claim. A very ambitious challenge. I hope we aren't setting those sights for our little one!' Rama's eyes danced as he spoke.

'Oh, Rama! Forever teasing me. But after all the fuss, a girl was born, a king met her and as the prophecy unfolded . . .'

'So, what is the point of the story?' said Rama with affection, as he delicately slurped his creamy dessert.

'Simply that the ritual of telling is a wish. It gives hope. Hope is what every human being thrives on whether they are wretched or rich. Stories, apart from giving hope, must be told and shared so everyone can try to understand the experience of life from another point of view,' replied Sita matter-of-factly.

'Wonderfully put!' Rama drank the cool water laced with sarsaparilla.

Just as he finished his last course and washed his hands in the gold finger bowl, Sita brought out the sweetened fennel. A minister came in, very apologetic, and explained that Rama had to tend to a court matter urgently that afternoon.

Rama returned in the late afternoon to the Assembly Hall. Urmilla was gathering the special herbs and bark from the courtyard that she had left to dry in the sun for a new supply of ointments for Sita. She could see Rama leaving the palace, winding his way from the pond full of lotuses towards the Grand Assembly Hall. Lakshmana was off on a mission to meet the hunters who brought news of changes in the migratory patterns of birds, so Rama was by himself. Urmilla noticed that over the last few days he looked more the Rama she had once known. He was getting used to the thought of a child in their midst, Sita had told her. Rama knelt and held his hands out to a male swan that came gliding at some speed, summoned by a king. The smell of clay wafted in the air as the afternoon breeze rose from the river. There was a moment of stillness to know that this could well be a happy time before jubilations, celebrations and all the anticipatory preparations for the birth of the royal.

By the time the cows returned to their herds, the dust was rising. Urmilla was standing in her garden on the western side that faced the palace garden pond. She marvelled at the way the lotuses opened with the first fingers of light at sunrise and gradually began to fold before sunset. The sun was turning crimson and the grove on the far western side of her compound wall looked dark with the foray of the banyan tree's branches. The bank sloped and her attention was diverted by the sunset, when she heard two men talking. One of them was clearly distressed.

She edged closer to the wall and could see an old man pleading with a youth, 'Please, take my daughter back.' Urmilla could tell by their dialect that they were dhobis, washermen.

'Why did she leave in the first place?' hissed the young man. 'Does she not know once she steps into my house, that is her place?'

'I beg you, forgive her, she is still a child at heart,' the father continued.

'Well, a child is afraid of the dark. But she walked out in the middle of the night.'

'What could she do? You beat her so hard, she was bleeding, she was afraid . . .'

'That I would kill her! Yes, I wish I had. At least I would have saved my honour! What will people say—she walked out like a prostitute!'

'Oh, please, please.' The old man could stand no longer. He knelt and said, 'Don't say that, we brought her up with the utmost care. She looks upon Sitadevi as her protector!' He broke down, choked by grief.

The son-in-law snarled. 'Well, I believe in honour in the old way, not like our king. Just look at him. What face does he have among men? He just took his wife back after she had been kept by Ravana for more than a year! Who knows what happened there? Get out of my way, you old fool!' And the old man stumbled, splayed face down, crying in the darkness and the wet mud. A dislodged stone scurried into the water with a splash.

Urmilla felt a pang of pity for the old man. Disgusted by the son-in-law's attitude, she returned to her apartments, resolving to seek the fellow out and knock some sense into his head. She was incensed. So these rumours were still flying about? Rumour and public opinion were faceless enemies, she thought. She would talk it over with Lakshmana. How could she tell Rama and Sita? She decided she would wait till Sita returned from her visit to the hermitage. Sita's trip was planned for the next day and Lakshmana was to escort her to the forest.

By the time Sita and Lakshmana left for the forest, Urmilla had begun to get her servants to interrogate all the dhobis in the area. She had to be discreet. She asked them to find out how many dhobis' daughters had been married over the last few months.

Because of this, she missed her daily routine of visiting Sita with soaked almonds and having their daily chat. 'It won't be long, Sita will be back by Dasami. There will be so much to catch up on. Meanwhile, Lakshmana will bring me news about her,' she consoled herself. As the still night progressed, she kept reliving the scene she had witnessed in the fading light the day before. What she did not know was that someone else had been there too. She had only heard the splash of water.

Her lids were heavy, but, during all these years, she had begun to dream with her eyes wide open. She composed poetry about waiting. She had begun a way of communicating with Lakshmana through her spirit. In that arc of fourteen years, when both were exiled from each other, he too communicated with her. But tonight sleep descended, and there was silence.

Rama

Rama lost his foothold. A stone had got dislodged and Rama could not break its fall. It bounced. With the sheer volition of its speed matched by its weight, the force of gravity and the downward slope of the bank, the stone made a splash—the way actions create consequences.

Rama had stopped by the grove of fragrant mango trees as he would whenever there was an opportunity to watch the sunset. The place was unchanged since the time he and his brothers used to swing from the branches as Dasaratha, their father, watched over them. Like a sports instructor, their father would assess which son had stronger arms while swinging from the branches, who was more nimble-footed, running along a high branch like a tightrope walker, and then invent new games. After the climbing, jumping, rolling and chasing, the boys would be led by Dasaratha to sit on the bank and watch what he called 'the miracle of each and every day', the sunset. Once he held Rama close and said, 'Look how the sun is sinking in the west. When you see that big ball of red nearly half gone, then wish with all your heart for the thing you want, and it will come true. You know why? Because that is the fire point, the purest moment. The sun is fire; you will never know anything more intense and pure than that!' Rama, whose name signified 'moving towards', remembered it, not for his father's romantic science, but for the moment when, like at the close of day all things point to night, he felt that closeness with his brothers, his life being swathed by the love and guardianship of an admirable father and accomplished king. Returning to the grove, often without Sita, was a remembrance of things past, when life was founded on the magic of innocence and wonder. Standing there, with the ghosts of the past reconciled, watching the sunset was an elixir for daily renewal. Even if things went wrong, he found new resolve by gazing at these sunsets. The blaze of light before it was consumed by night brought hope that the sun would rise the next day, and what was left incomplete could be put right. Every sunset was different. Some days it was wide and clear and the fireball descending from gold to crimson to deep red would simmer with its heat waves as it slipped into the horizon. In that instant, the light changed the landscape. First illuminating every object, then, as the blaze faded, lighting the trees, buildings, livestock, people, everything seemed to be sculpted of ebony. On other days, clouds splayed the light across all directions and became iconic of the power that gave life. Its light touched everything; it was the symbol of royalty. To Rama, in his wheel of life—a continuous play of unanticipated shocks—the sun was the only constant. Gazing at the sun he would recall the strands of poems from the *Isha Upanishad*:

> The face of the truth is hidden by thy golden orb, O sun.
> That do thou remove, in order that I who am devoted to truth may behold its glory.
> O Nourisher, only seer, controller of all—O illumining sun, fountain of life for all creatures—withhold thy light, gather together thy rays. May I behold through thy grace thy most blessed form.
> The Being that dwells therein—even that Being am I.

Sita had been planning her trip to the forest for the next morning and the household was in preparation for months since she had announced it. It was her way of offering thanks to the friends in the forest and to Valmiki before she gave birth, as she knew her life would take a different turn when she came back. She would settle into the role of a mother, wife and queen. Rama, too, felt it was a good idea. Sita's mother had died of grief on hearing about Sita's abduction, muttering in her last breath, 'What will people say?' Now Valmiki and the forest were Sita's family. Rama understood her need for parental warmth.

The evening before Sita's departure he couldn't resist stopping by the grove on his way from court. The sun was setting and this time he really had something to wish for. Not so much to wish for as to be grateful for. Sita was back in his life, and each day dissolved one more layer of caution and reserve till hopefully, one day, they would return to their former selves, and the trust they shared when they married would be restored. After fourteen years they were going to have a child. All those years in exile, they had entwined themselves in each other's thoughts and could not tell each other apart. But the year that Sita was abducted, so many new worlds came into existence. Rama met Hanuman and that friendship shaped tangible worlds, like armies, but also intangible ones like courage and unfailing service.

That was when Rama heard voices. He drew back under the shade of a tree. The father-in-law and son-in-law were too involved in their argument to notice they were being watched. Rama was about to intervene, not as a king handing out justice, but as a mediator, enabling each party to see the other's point of view and arriving at a reconciliation before a solution. It had won him a place in the hearts of everyone he had met in his years of exile. He found it was the best way of knowing a case and understanding his people even after he returned to court and was crowned king.

But at the mention of Sita, a cold pang of fear clutched his heart. The son-in-law's snarl kept ringing in his head: 'Well, I believe in honour in the old way, not like our king . . . He just took his wife back after she had been kept by Ravana for more than a year! Who knows what happened there?' Rama's legs were like stone pillars, his arms heavy boulders and his tongue a frozen river. A part of him became a wild beast, ready to bash the young man into a pulp. Not kill him, because the ensuing silence would only magnify the words the murdered man had uttered, as they would remain suspended in the air. Another part of Rama was baying like a wounded animal at the sight of its mate gorged by other animals. Every fibre in Rama's body tingled with rage as he stretched and tightened the fabric of rationality, like damp leather on the ring of a drum. He kept tapping and toning his mind with discursive thoughts of ethics, purpose, governance, tradition and the state, including the collective good. No mantras alleviated the pain screaming in and tearing at his heart.

What the son-in-law said hung like spit in the air and the old man, broken by the ammunition of words, was splayed on the bank beating his fists as his tears and saliva mixed with the mud. Rama walked away and the stone tumbled from its nest of roots. It splashed and formed widening rings as it plunged to the bottom of the palace's lotus pond. Each of the three men had reached their thresholds of endurance. In the scheme of things to come, what began as a domestic quarrel in a washerman's hut outside the palace would create ever-widening rings of influence in the royal household, in turn affecting the course of history.

Rama returned to his palace trembling. He went straight to his map room, avoiding the main entrance. He sent word through his trusted courtier for Lakshmana to meet him immediately. He knew this was difficult as Lakshmana was on a secret-service mission with hunters, who acted as the king's spies, and there was no way of contacting him until he returned at night. Dismissing all his servants Rama decided to be alone. He would wait. However long that took. He knew what it meant to wait. He also knew that when waiting, one's thoughts and feelings rushed like a river, breaking the banks and shifting the vantage points of a landscape.

He began unfurling the scrolls of new maps that defined the boundaries of his kingdom and those of his neighbours. So far there had been no disputes, and it was due to the diligence of Bharata who, over the years of Rama's exile, had served the kingdom and the domestic needs of its people with great attention to detail. Thoughts of expansion, even through trade, were not part of Bharata's scheme. In fact, Bharata had no ambition to rule and had done so only on Rama's insistence. On his return and after the coronation, Rama was advised that in the foreseeable future there would be shortages of natural and other resources within the kingdom. Unless there was some kind of expansion of territories that provided those resources, Ayodhya would become dependent; a dependent kingdom is vulnerable to attack. The lines on the map were blurring. Rama's dilemma was now concrete: should he focus on the external demands of the state before he weeded out the internal discontent among his people? Both made the kingdom, his state, vulnerable.

He had always believed that the state and the individual functioned like the human heart—a circulation system of codes formed by people's consent and well communicated at all levels—where each enabled the other to perform at optimum level. What was in the minds of individuals eventually influenced collective action. It came to be written 'to each according to his ability'—that was the building block of the social constitution. The principle was a good one. Based on the human anatomy, limbs and organs dispersed functions that were carried out as a unified action of the body.

A thought was an atom. It fuelled energy that could be used either way—for darkness or light. He had experienced it during exile, wandering and meeting all kinds of people. He knew his people and their circumstances. They entrusted him to uphold not only what was materially beneficial to them but also the spiritual goal and purpose in life—that which made life bearable amidst vicissitudes. Rama believed in an open channel of communication with his people, not so much to please them as to contextualize the legislation of each individual's dharma—or right action. What nourished the individual would replenish the state. Rama had brought about considerable change from his father's time—the most significant of which was reserving the love and honour of one wife.

Hearing the washerman hurl such abuse in the name of Sita both dismayed and enraged him. Had she not proved her mettle in that trial by fire? Did he not arrange it so everyone could see with their own eyes what he knew her to be? And how much had been at stake—including the prospect of losing her completely—when he had uttered those words. They had sounded so strange on his tongue: 'Sita! Ravana is dead. You are free to go now.' And then the horror lurched again. Was Ravana really dead? How he still continued to cause havoc! Ravana was a great creator of illusions. What if these shards of doubt were also his creation? These thoughts like fine crystals of poison were foreign to Rama, but, unnoticed by him, they dissolved in his mind. And now Sita was with child. Was that an illusion as well? Was Ravana hovering to see that if not in life, then by his death he could separate Rama and Sita? How intense must be the power of his love for Sita.

Rama knew that Sita never uttered the name Ravana. He had accepted her silence as her way of recovering from that traumatic captivity. He knew from the depth of his being that Sita was true to him, as Rama knew he was true to her. They were two bodies entwined around one soul. Did he not see how her eyes blazed when for one brief instant she stood apart from him at the trial of fire—that she would give up her life were she to be separated from his belief in her? Did she not say 'Ra and Ma were the only two syllables I knew in all my time in captivity; it was all my breath uttered when I inhaled, exhaled and inhaled again; it was Rama who kept me alive'? Then why was this shadow still looming over them?

That day when he found Sita beside her dowry chest, he saw the look in her eyes; she could feel the hurt that overwhelmed him for one blinding moment. She had been about to speak, but he turned to go. Even then he had heard her say 'Rama . . .', caught mid-sentence, and he hadn't stayed to listen. Now the moment had passed, and he had decided on a different course of action.

Sita was tinkling the little bell for the evening aarti.

The musical instruments were being tuned, and Rama could hear the drum throbbing like a heartbeat. He calmly strode past the columns and entered the hall as everyone faced the ancestral deities and Sita waved the lamps. The air was thick with the fragrance of sandalwood. The lead sang in perfect pitch and rhythm. She led and the chorus followed, all hearts and minds singing in unison. Rama and Sita looked at each other for one moment as the subjects thanked the ancestral gods for their king and their queen. Sita smiled such a heavenly smile; a warm wave of love and reassurance washed over him.

After the evening meal Rama spent some time with Sita who told him about the allocation of gifts for the journey. He then returned to his map room before retiring. Lakshmana was waiting. The attendants knew that when the brothers met, they had to be left alone. When the last footfall was heard fading away, Lakshmana pulled out the palm-leaf message he had received and looked at Rama, 'What does this mean?'

'You do know we are leaving tomorrow?' Rama came forward to calm Lakshmana as he had done for all the years he had known him.

'No, Rama. I cannot understand you. You who have understood the essence of the *Upanishads*, who seek the truth in all things? Rama, it was you who taught me that Brahman is in everything. Not just the eye but in what makes one see. Not just the strength in one's arms and legs but the impulse that makes them move. Not just the thinking of our thoughts but the essence of how we make them dark or bright. Not just the heart as a vital organ but as one that contains a luminous flower; to know that it holds the eternal self, which is the size of a thumb. You know the subtle currents of the seventy-three nerves that rest at sleep to wake in the finite world. You know the difference between dreaming and waking, and the wakeful eternal. All this, in the darkest times, you have breathed in words more eloquent than song. All this is contained in you. With my eyes and heart I have seen and lived and believed this of you. Even Hanuman held that the love Sita and you have for each other is beyond all things finite, the embodiment of all ideals. That love kept us wakeful during our exile to what is good and what leads to evil. Rama, listen to me. Above all, people know that you see Brahman, shining like a million sunsets when you meditate. You are the embodiment of Brahman, like a profound artist touched by the genius of play and awakening, who can see the birth of new life in dead wood. Why are you falling prey to rumour? You are above this!'

'This is not rumour. It is about challenging power with principle. If I don't put myself through this test, how will everyone know that we are all subject to the principle. Can't you see, we are all bound by the rules?

'Even the infinite is contained in the finite. If we are to bring about change then we have to take the first step. People will learn to see the truth. Ideals at all cost must be held high. Did we not endure so much because we believed in unravelling the ultimate potential of what makes the human divine? Whoever we are, sacrifice is inevitable.'

'But you cannot wash away what everyone is thinking and does not dare to say. It's impossible. Will your action not prove that Sita is guilty? And Sita? Does she know she is at the centre of this?'

'She is central to everything. She will understand,' said Rama conclusively.

When Rama returned to his apartments, Sita was asleep. He lay down beside her. She stirred and in her sleep murmured his name. He held her close, placing his hand on her belly. The foetus was kicking. Rama cupped his hand, holding on to the movement of life before birth; consciousness of what was unconscious. Sita was his. How could he ever doubt that? Ravana created his delusions, but Sita could never be swayed. Of that Rama was certain. Whatever the price, all he wanted was for his people to see her the way she really was.

Valmiki

Valmiki had taken to sweeping of late. Sweeping around his hut, and then in a circle defining the hermitage. He swept the clearing in front of the huts that was for visiting ascetics. In the centre of the clearing was a step-high square, and another angled square on top of it making a base in the shape of an eight-point star for lighting the fire. Branches, logs, twigs, dried leaves were all stacked beyond the circle, to the right. A wooden cauldron and terracotta pots and pitchers were beside the stack. Two goats and a cow and her calf sat at the far end facing the back of the dwellings.

Valmiki swept leaves, seeds, crushed fruit, bird droppings, peacock feathers, snail shells, snake skins, weeds, worms, anything that his broom—made from a brush of thorny leaves and twigs tied to a branch—could find in its path.

He swept through tangled thoughts, ideas, dilemmas, predicaments, half-heard stories in his head. He brushed patterns on the earth that swirled in concentric circles, looking like giant fingerprints. He whispered in musical sounds and fragments of poems, muttered eulogies, coined aphorisms, composed mantras, tapped percussive variations on the broomstick and swept his mind free of alien thoughts. What kept seeping through the cracks of his mind, through the creative fissures, were the ideas for characters who would be written into his stories.

As Valmiki swept, he populated his imagination with people. Characters who were real, historical, legendary and imagined. He tugged through the tangled, hair-splitting dilemma of what was more important in telling a story— character or plot? He was now dealing with real emotions, lives, people whose stories, even if it was not their intention, inspired other lives, generations, histories—over centuries, across continents. He placed them in struggles that were domestic, personal and spiritual, as well as political, because he felt it was his characters' due. But it wasn't just right action that his characters had to think about. It was also the tangled web of emotions they had to comb through. Valmiki discovered that the adventure of life was not about unravelling destiny; it was about unravelling the constellation of thoughts, emotions and will.

Then there was the one unaccounted thing—grace. Whether or not one believed in what was commonly known as god, there was still grace. A consciousness that was memory and beyond, primeval and eternal, computed and random, accidental but structured. On the sides of a human forehead sat its temples. Concealed from the outside, these temples were portals to that intense experience which connected daily impressions and information from the sense organs to knowledge. These connections flowed in a current that danced in light from an eternal source, refracted like the rainbow from a prism and flowed into other sources. The sensation was not of repetition. It was a swirling, shimmering pool for the inner eye that buoyed in the centre of the chest. At the core of the human, this consciousness, or grace, was a luminous flower. To see it, touch it, be it, was to be immortal. When the nanosecond of total connectivity had passed, a wave of longing to once again belong to 'that' would surge.

Valmiki often asked himself what this feeling of great beauty and the longing to belong was about. During his wanderings between cities and forests, he would see temples. *Who are they for?* The answer was a name, a god. *Had anyone seen god?* No; god in the form of a woman or man or child or animal appeared in a dream and told people what to seek or do.

In cities and towns the stones were in the shape of a human, worshipped as god. And, as he wandered on, there were hunters, travellers, villagers, tribals who would, on seeing stone lingams sprouting from the earth, wash them, adorn them with flowers, leaves, vermilion and offer them love. Among forest people, there were no great incantations, but a cry that ululated from the heart. Words were passed on, each becoming a sign to unlock the door to the portal going deeper within where everything was connected. Darkness could be seen being forced away, and a chink of light would emerge from it like a sabre. It was a sure sign, like a number, a symbol of pure mathematics that connected the gross with the subtle within a second. Valmiki had gone through the experience of inhabiting that nanosecond of allness. Coming out of it meant encountering the world with its variety, its gods, with or without gender, multiplicity, words, languages, caste, divisions, subdivisions, categories, qualities, difference. Many hermits and ascetics, who had experienced this allness, chose not to return. They wanted more and more of that immersion.

Valmiki remembered, all too clearly, his past as a highwayman before he became a poet. The test that Narada had put him through about the fragility of human relationships was severe but revealing. It was the first thing he could recall to offer Sita some comfort from that first shock of abandonment she felt when Lakshmana rode away with Rama's order for her exile. Valmiki was merely an ascetic; he knew the labyrinth of human love and bitterness, the tactile bonds that gently enmesh the individual and the nagging hangover of a belief that there was freedom on the horizon. He had turned inward in the quest for that freedom.

How much of this Valmiki had touched and tasted, struggled and danced with, cried and shouted about with song. Now he was at a loss. He was the one who had chosen to traverse both worlds—of human longing and the longing for cosmic allness. He wanted to write that story of infinite possibilities within a lifetime.

His characters had taken over. They had been born. They were flesh and blood. They travelled with the speed of light. Valmiki gave them situations, but they took on actions driven by their impulses. Did he want to portray them or did he want to get under their skin and tell the story from their point of view? He was in a dilemma.

Suddenly, he saw a woman approaching. Although her hair was shorn and she was wrapped in white, like a disciple out on a mission to seek a guru, her body, as it moved, still had impressions of a woman who was beautiful and knew a courtly life. She carried a staff and an earthen pot for collecting alms. Her skin still shone; there was nothing of the withered ascetic about her, but she had the look of desperation that gave her the intensity of a ritual performer. She had not yet caught sight of Valmiki. And he wasn't aware he was staring at her. She was the prey not of a man but an artist. He was taking in everything about her and trying to piece together a life story, reflecting on the gulf between her appearance and its reality.

What the woman saw was a large shadow, loose hair, with an extension from its body which, in her fright, she could not recognize as a broomstick. She could not see Valmiki's face clearly but his gaze pierced like a laser through her veil of inattentiveness and she became suddenly aware of his presence. She screamed and fell face down. Sita rushed out of her dwelling, with another female hermit and when they turned the intruder's body, limp but breathing, Sita too screamed.

Sita wept, kissed the eyebrows of the woman on the ground, laughed, wept again, wiped her nose and the saliva from her lips as she cried open-mouthed. 'Urmi, Urmi, Urmi . . .' she repeated like a child with a rag doll, rocking the intruder's body and then breaking into an incantatory chant, which flowed into a lament and then burst into a celebratory song. Valmiki was stunned, as was the attendant. For a moment he wondered whether after all this time, Sita could endure no more and was giving way to hallucinations. Sita looked up. 'This is my Urmi, my sister, friend, Lakshmana's wife, my sister-in-law!' As she uttered the words, so many reels of memories flickered before her eyes, as if she were seeing their lives flash past.

'Urmi, wake up ma, please . . . don't leave me! You are my home, my hope . . . please open your eyes. You found us, how can you not see us now . . . please,' Sita pleaded. The attendant brought some water and Sita sprinkled it on the woman. It was Urmilla. But what had happened to her hair, her jewellery, her way of dressing like a younger queen? Valmiki brought a paste of pungent-smelling leaves and, rubbing it in his palms, cupped it over Urmilla's nose. Muscles twitched around her eyebrows, her eyes watered and, sneezing, she catapulted into consciousness. The first face she saw was Valmiki's and before she could convulse in horror again, she heard Sita: 'Oh! Urmi, my darling Urmi! My Urmi!' Valmiki and the attendant withdrew with a feeling of immense satisfaction that a life had been saved and that two sisters were reunited.

It was good to see Sita so happy. After she got over the shock of being banished—that was the formal court order, but she really had been abandoned—each hour Valmiki watched her chipping away at her grief for the sake of the life not yet born. Sometimes she would give in to the burden of grief. There was no death, so there was no body, no tangible object that had been lost. In her heart and head swirled an ocean of remembrances strung on love, struggle, endeavour and faith, but now it was doubt that dismembered so many images from the past. Like the time when Rama would gaze at the full moon he would always hold her and say: 'This is our wishing point. How many lives and loves the moon has seen; we will see a thousand and one full moons together—our love as radiant and timeless.' That would have accounted for sixty years of married life. But they had barely seen fifteen years together; and while the moon continued its radiance in its orbit, a ring of coldness and silence encircled her heart.

She wanted to pour in thoughts about Rama into her empty heart. She wanted to create a fingerprint that stretched like a mural of parenthood across the blank canvas of the newborn's consciousness. When she tried and made some headway, she would immediately start to question herself if it were a lie. She wanted this child to be alerted to truth, the rawness of nature; not the forest but the vicious coldness of the human mind. With the sudden appearance of Urmilla, that cold orbit of silence within Sita broke open.

Even though it had been a few weeks, Urmi and Sita felt they had been apart for years. There was so much catching up to do. Valmiki was relieved as the time for the childbirth was approaching. He had known of childbirths when he had a home, as a highwayman in the forest. But it seemed as if women did this naturally. He wavered at what kind of assistance he could provide, but now that Urmilla was here all those apprehensions lifted and he decided to make lodgings for both women.

Sita waited till Urmilla had recovered from her journey. She kept stroking her shaven head and wondered why Urmilla had cut off her long, long hair.

'I waited for Lakshmana to return,' began Urmilla, 'and on the day he was to return, Rama sent me a message saying he was delayed. Seemed strange to send me a message, but some delegation had come, so I thought Rama was caught up in that and without you there, he would be looking into the arrangements in greater detail.

'The next day passed and the same thing happened. I was worried because I wanted to know if something had happened to you and Lakshmana on the journey. When I tried to see Rama, it was impossible. He surrounded himself with his guards, and soon I noticed there were more guards around our house. I was constantly questioned about where I was going and when I would return. It was for my safety, they said, without any further explanations. By the fourth day there were armed guards. If I mentioned Lakshmana's name, it was as if he were a legend. Revered but never spoken of. I tried to question the servants, and they were soon put on different shifts or dismissed. There was no way out for me. I had to leave because I thought I would go mad. What had happened to Lakshmana? To you and, indeed, to Rama? I thought if I left from the front of the house, I would be followed. I didn't know where to go any more. At first I thought I would go and seek Rama out. But it seemed as if the guards had been ordered to protect him from me!

'There was just one of my trusted servants left. I feigned sickness and a sprained back. So the servant brought the old gnarled masseuse. We began evening massage treatments and broths steamed and stank up the house through every room. To get to that condition, since I was being inspected each day, I had to do several things: starve, get diarrhoea, be convincingly weak, conserve enough energy so I could be alert to any chance of escape. I had prepared myself that any evening could be the one. But the shift of the guards was never regular or timed. One night, three weeks ago, I cut my hair and exchanged clothes with the old woman; I carried her in a bundle on my back past the guards and out of the house. That whole night I walked dressed as a bhikshu, begging alms and travelling, meandering, mingling among pilgrims, sleeping anywhere and not daring to ask directions to Valmiki's hermitage. I edged my way out.'

'But you've tricked them successfully, Urmi. Now you're safe. They will not be looking for you here.'

50

Valmiki was immersed in his thoughts. 'Just when I thought I had swept aside all possibilities of adding more characters. Here's a seed that has sprouted with infinite branches creating infinite probabilities!' But he was also aware that now he was the only man in the hermitage with three women, and not all of them on a mission of spiritual learning. In fact, now he was the disciple of women, learning how they lived life.

The most important thing was that Sita and Urmilla needed to be together. So, after Urmilla regained her strength, she, along with the attendant and Valmiki, began to build a hut.

A couple of months later, at two in the morning, Sita woke uneasily and tugged at the rope next to her that had been tied to the beam. Urmilla leapt up and got the attendant to bring a wreath of leaves and soft grass. Water was always on the boil. Urmilla felt around Sita's belly to determine where the foetus's head was, as Sita convulsed in pain. Both women lifted Sita's torso and guided her leg by leg to step on to the wooden frames on either side. Within the outer wooden frames were wooden stirrups and the wreath of leaves and soft grass was placed on the floor. This was swathed in several pieces of cloth. Sita was given ropes in both her hands that were suspended from the beams. As she stood on the wooden stirrups and pulled the ropes, she heaved, and with a gush her water burst with an explosion of blood and mucus. Urmilla's midwifery included soothing Sita and calming the terrified ascetic attendant who was witnessing how life comes ripping and tearing through flesh into the predawn darkness of a busy morning in the forest. Amidst Sita's intermittent ear-splitting screams and howls, the women cheered her on:

O lovely Sitamma! Tie your hair in one breath
In the next let it down
This way we can count
How many breaths it takes to bring our long-awaited
guest's arrival.

You are a queen, a mother who brings this one in
Sure as night brings the day.
From the ocean of warm darkness where you held
this one
Now from those swirling waters this one has come to
play.

Sitamma, Sitamma, you can endure a while longer;
Tie your hair in one breath
In the next let it down
This way we can count . . .

Valmiki was sitting outside, as he did when he had to think of words shaping an idea. But his heart was racing. Birth for a man is so different. It is the soft footfall of an idea that can easily go missing. No surface, texture, smell or volume. But from the women's hut he could hear screams, laughter and songs and what would emerge would be a full body—hopefully with breath as with blood. With the birth of an idea he had to build its muscle with words, find phrases that made for blood, sentences that gave skin, grammar that gave guts, vocabulary that gave weight, sound that gave breath and voice, irony that afforded insight; but he wondered how did one create the testicles, penis, vulva and vagina to make for the sex of an idea? A woman holds an entire epic in her womb, brings it out and it speaks for itself! When this realization dawned, Sita had been in labour for nearly two hours.

By four the singing had escalated into a frenzied game cheering. Valmiki began seeing things through the dark. The owl had been hooting and he had heard it between the screams, almost reassuring him that his nightscape would return to normal. Women had entered his life and things had been turned upside down. A part of him enjoyed the challenge. Suddenly, he saw a luminous figure in the clearing, about to enter the women's hut. He wore a silk dhoti, his forehead beamed and the sandal-paste mark was prominent. His feet barely touched the ground. In one hand he held a string of pearls and in the other, a stylus.

'Brahma!' Valmiki uttered, hardly able to say the name. He bowed low at the figure's feet. 'I am impressed that you should be able to see me, Valmiki. So much is happening now, eh? What with births and exiles . . . hmm?' said Brahma.

'But, O Great One, this is your hour between sleeping and waking, the profound moment of creation. I am so honoured you have graced this hermitage.'

'Well, I'm on my way to see the child. He is born.'

Valmiki blinked. 'Of course, Great One. Could you grant me one favour?'

'Depends on what it is. I'm economical with boons.'

'Would you tell me what is the karma of this child who has such a great ancestry?' asked Valmiki.

'It is difficult.'

'But you are the one who writes everyone's karma! How can you . . .' Valmiki was indignant.

'Don't hold me responsible. Ancestry is merely social and material reality. I take account of what thoughts rippled through one's last moments in the previous life. That's what makes them choose the location of their next life. What have I got to do with this child's difficulty?'

Valmiki only said, 'Narayana, Narayana!'

Brahma reasoned: 'Why call on Narayana? Ask yourself—whenever you have conceived a character, have you ever been able to control their karma? Is creation about structure or control from your point of view?'

The luminous figure glided on the owl's wings as it flew across the clearing to its favourite tree.

Lava

The first memory was never about words. It was sensation. Sleep in a warm fluid. Swimming. Kick-dancing, ever buoyant. It was perhaps dark, but then it was a great and deep sleep with some fleeting impressions on a mind not yet conscious. Sound? Yes. The first consciousness of not being alone. Or a sense of a presence around and out there. It was the sound of ticking. Ti-dhik, ti-dhik, ti-dhik, and on and on it went through the timeless swimming, with each instant, as the tiny body grew cell by cell with sap from Sita's body. Then there was a voice that was familiar and constant. Sita's humming. Resonant and rising from the depths with a musical air. The familiarity with the sound started a chord of communication for the tiny body when it heard the hum, and, like a snake charmed by a piper's melody, it would pause from the great float and kick-dance. Sita would place her hand on her belly sometimes with laughter or would say, 'Did you enjoy that? Want to hear some more? What would you like for dinner tonight?' and the call-response of words from the outside in and kick-dancing from within to the outside would start again. It was the primal choreography of sound rhythms and foot flexes as dance, and an eternal dialogue of heartbeats and the motion of life.

The brave new arrival into the world was dependent on the ripening of all body cells. Sita's body was ready to release this configuration of a complete body from a dark, warm, fluid interior to an exterior of air and light. The head coming out through a contracting and expanding cave-shaped ring of flesh. For the tiny body, its eyes shut tight, it was sound alone that marked the first difference between the experience of the interior and the exterior.

What a whirr, so different from the sound of the eternal swimming. Only later would he come to know they were human voices crying, singing and cheering, happy and exhausted. Then a tight slap on his back. It was the first trauma of air and sensation and flinching skin—a great change from being inside fluid and floating. The tiny body's eyes opened. Now the sensation had changed, and it was of the warmth of a human hand, of being held. The tiny body, all crinkly, was being wiped clean as it screamed and kicked at all the dryness; having come out of a snug wet interior, this felt too prickly and dry. With his first gulp of air, the one sensation that took over all else was hunger.

Hunger was screaming within him; the hunger to live. As the boy came into life, screaming in affirmation, his inner eye opened. The space he entered was bathed in light, and standing in the doorway was a luminous figure who touched the boy's forehead. From that moment on the boy named Lava always saw a white luminous dot between his brows. He also remembered the moment his eyes first opened when he was born, and at times the sensation of swimming before his birth. As the luminous figure left, Lava heard around him the sound of ocean waves like the fluttering of owl wings. He saw his mother Sita's face. The moment she took him in her hands and soothed his tiny, trembling body, holding him up to her face, and started humming *Om Namo Narayana*, he could recognize the resonant hum from when he was inside. His being registered this touch as *home*, safe from all others and embedded it in his memory as 'Amma'.

'Sita,' said Urmilla, overcome with emotion, 'he is every bit like the sun, born at the break of dawn. He will dispel every kind of darkness.'

'Yes, my lovely darling will hold up truth like a mirror! May that always be your armour!' replied Sita exhilarated, forgetting the agony and exhaustion of her labour till a few moments ago. She was made to lie down with her baby. With cloths soaked in warm water and turmeric, Urmilla and the attendant sponged Sita and the newborn. Hot milk laced with turmeric and crushed pepper was brought and Sita drank it eagerly holding on to her baby, lying face down on top of her. With the birdsong of early morning, her racing heart started to slow down, the milk and turmeric soothed her throat, and with a feeling of lightness and joy, and a heaviness in her body she slept, smiling.

The morning hours passed in bursts of sleep for Urmilla as she watched over Sita, the attendant and even Valmiki. In the hour before midday, the visiting deer, the goats, the cow and her calf heard a shrill cry. From the haze of sleep everyone jumped up. The raw cry of hunger spiralled from the women's hut making the leaves shiver in the warm breeze. The realization that life in the hermitage would be changed forever dawned on Valmiki as he decisively walked, then hesitated, then moved towards the women's hut as the birth had been announced to him. He had not seen the newborn yet. As he approached the hut he was waved away vigorously by Urmilla: 'Sita's giving the first feed! I'll tell you when is a good time to come.'

Valmiki was indignant, but after years of discovering how events change human responses, he smiled wisely and withdrew. He witnessed his reaction: 'How dare she! She is a guest here and now she is dictating when I can and cannot see Sita! Am I to be treated as a stranger in my own hermitage?' He began to hear the same phrase from another corridor of thought in his head: 'Sita has just given birth and is exhausted; Urmilla is the only one who can tend to her needs. Why am I interfering with thoughts of power, about who is playing host and who is the guest? What a terrific and unexpected stroke of genius in the grand accident of life that Urmilla should appear at the time of Sita's labour. What could I have done? Who could have predicted that Sita would be exiled? It has changed the whole course of the story and, so many lives.'

Inside the hut, the newborn was gorging on Sita's breast secreting the ivory-coloured, sweet milk-sap of life. Sita's heart danced with happiness. Urmilla and Sita laughed at the way the infant made smacking and chortling sounds as he suckled. Sita stroked his tiny head of jet black hair, saying, 'May you never be in want of anything. Let your heart and mind always be your best friends in life.'

'He certainly has strong lungs! So he will know how to shout and get whatever he wants,' said Urmilla cheerfully.

Valmiki entered the hut when Sita was ready to receive him. He bowed low with folded hands, saluting the newborn. He could see the signs of Brahma's visit in the luminous dot on the infant's forehead. The tiny window of the hut brought in a draft of fresh air and the dazzling sun streamed on the heads of mother and son, thick with blue-black hair. 'Well, Maharaj! You picked a fine spot for a hermitage! Now it has become a township!' was Sita's welcoming remark.

'What better way to contemplate Truth than by applying all of life's variations to experience the Veda, heh? So, you are well, Sita? What have you named the child?'

'Lava. I hope he and I can have a home here. It is true I don't have a home, but I want this boy to be learned and who could be a better guru than you, Maharaj? Urmilla and I . . .'

'Done! You don't have to say another word, Sita. He may not learn the ways of the court, but he will learn to tell the story of Truth,' said Valmiki emphatically, wiping his tears.

So, within a few days everyone was getting into a new routine that at first seemed all-consuming and centred on Lava's hunger patterns. But soon, everyday rituals were threaded together with making the fire, cooking, feeding, washing, listening to thoughts of the day, singing, debating and hosting pilgrims and, occasionally, travellers.

The days passed into months and it was already time for the rice-milk ceremony for Lava. His head had been shaved of his bee-black curly hair, but within a few days the stubble emerged like an indigo wash. His eyes were blue-black and he buzzed with a curiosity about everything that moved or was still. His hearing was impeccable and he could repeat the exact tone and pitch of what he heard, even if he could not pronounce complete words properly.

He had a large vocabulary to draw from. The wind in the trees, soft rain, hard rain on the huts, lightning, rolling thunder, water pouring into vessels, crackling fire, the snap of dry branches and sticks, the cow mooing, the calf calling, goats bleating, the plopping and patting of dung cakes, the difference between wet and dry wood being chopped, Valmiki sweeping the hermitage, the shy arrival and departure of deer as they munched on leaves. With human sounds the repertoire was limited to the people around him. He could catch the high notes of Sita's humming, the cackling of Valmiki's laughter, Urmilla's throaty and nasal voice and the attendant's whispers. The passing travellers never stayed long enough and were often too tired or deferential in Valmiki's presence, but what Lava could understand was who made up his 'family' of humans and animals, and who were 'outsiders'.

The rice-milk ceremony was also a preparation for the first word to be inscribed on Lava's tongue with honey. Valmiki inscribed an *aa-au-mm* and so took on his youngest apprentice. 'There,' he said with his customary cheer, 'the three syllables that make for all dimensions of the world and the human body! But don't forget the silence after each cycle. That will teach you everything about this world and that, and how to tell it.' Lava only sucked the honey and put his hand in the leaf cup and licked his palm clean.

The merriment continued, but Sita held on to its sanctity as well. 'Imagine that!' she thought. 'Were Lava born in the kingdom, Rama and I would have sent for Valmiki for this auspicious rite! How naturally this has happened now—I wish Rama was here to see . . .' She had to stop herself. It seemed as if a former self was taking over. Was it natural to think of Rama with such closeness since he was the father of the child? After all, no woman can make a child all by herself. Was she weakening? Should she inform Rama about the birth of the child? But then, would Lava be taken away? It might mean that Lava would be in greater comfort and learn to be a prince were he to be sent to Rama in Ayodhya. But, if Rama remained obsessed with matters of the state, would he make any time for Lava? Wouldn't the child feel more abandoned amidst luxury without someone to love and guide him? What life was he being exposed to in the forest? Was she being selfish in not being able to part from him because he was the only joy she felt of late? Sita decided after all these apprehensions that Lava should stay with her, as in this forest he would have his mother's love, his aunt's and the attendant's care, and the tutelage of the great Valmiki, who would initiate him into the ways of enlightened learning the way no court scholar could. Lava was playing with a piece of wood that Urmilla had carved into a wheel. He was looking intently at Sita, and when she looked back she wondered how much of that decision was really hers? Does a soul really choose the family it wants to live in? Then wait in the womb of its choice to form a body? She had not said a word, but Lava felt the chord of communication. He pushed the wheel away and stood up bouncing and stretching his arms. Sita's heart was churning. She wiped her tears and picked up her son and, placing him on her hip, said: 'No more tears from me, Lava. Come, let us go and talk to that peepul leaf and see what she has to say.' Lava held her face on either side with his tiny hands on her ears. Sita looked into his face as if she were looking into a mirror, not just for her reflection, but for a quality of her being. Her son looked straight into her eyes, and with a toothless smile acknowledging her, kissed his mother's forehead.

One day, Urmilla had set off with the attendant to seek out some leaves and berries to create a health tonic for Lava. She also prepared vast quantities of it and stored it for willing travellers and pilgrims and they bartered it for grain and cloth. Sita was bathing Lava, and Valmiki was composing a new metre.

Sita had to wash clothes by the forest spring and return with some fresh water for drinking. She had counted on Lava being asleep after his feed and bath. However, that was not working to plan. She began to wonder if he had had an extra dose of Urmilla's health tonic as he was extremely energetic. Sita tried to play with him and tire him out but he seemed to be more vigorous and would not have her leave him. Sita couldn't help gazing at the sun's speeding journey towards midday. She didn't want to blame delays on Lava and wanted to keep everything just so by the time Urmilla and the attendant returned, as they never really got a break from daily chores. The heat was rising and Sita had tried every trick to get Lava to nap, but he tricked her back by pretending to sleep, and when he got wind that she wanted to go somewhere, he did everything to detain her without crying.

At last she went to Valmiki. 'Maharaj, it's getting late for my chores. Please, could you take Lava's lessons a little earlier?'

Valmiki could see Sita getting exasperated and that might mean putting up with an irritable woman in the hermitage, which could mean a really bad day for composition. He would constantly have to stay out of her way to keep his mind calm so that it would chime with the rhythm and metre for his poem. Valmiki had discovered early enough in life that passive resistance requires greater energy than confrontation. He had noticed that when women get exasperated they keep clearing things out or rearranging them, and this could entail the jangling sounds of pots and pans. He needed the heap of palm leaves in the chaotic order they seemed to be in to make the connections for his forthcoming poem. He was terrified almost like a child that Sita might get into a fit of clearing the chaos and stack all his palm leaves, written on or not, and he would completely lose the pattern of what he had in mind.

'No problem, Sita, leave Lava with me and we will pass the time. You go and do what you have to,' said Valmiki rather strategically as Sita lowered Lava on to his lap.

Sita left the hermitage with a bundle of clothes and a long pouch of the sweet-smelling but bitter reetha soap nuts. Valmiki saw her stop at the entrance to the hermitage, put the bundle down and retie her long hair into a topknot—something she always did before leaving and returning to the hermitage. To Valmiki, it seemed that she was conducting a little ritual, the way classical performers do before entering the dimension of imagined and heightened reality; of closure on one space before embarking into another. She always bit her lip and looked thoughtful, almost as if she would have to slip into another role as she left the hermitage or returned to it. Who was she when she went to do these tasks? An attendant at the hermitage? An abandoned wife and mother who was taking refuge? An exiled queen? Or a resourceful woman who lived as comfortably at the hermitage—with her companions doing the chores in rotation—as she would as a queen in a palace with an army of servants?

Lava had started tapping his toy rattle on Valmiki's knee. 'Tut-tut-tut,' Valmiki started and the child joined in the beat. 'Tat-tat-tvam asi,' said Valmiki clapping his hands and the child repeated, 'Ta-ta-tamaswee . . .' The game was good and Lava was engaged; slowly his eyes glazed and, with his hand in midair grasping the rattle, he fell fast asleep. Valmiki decided not to move him but lay him on the deerskin mat beside him. Valmiki watched him closely, and then he was struck by a phrase, which grew into a poem:

What mother could resist giving her child this sleep
Kissed by the dappled sun
Amidst the fragrance of shimmering neem leaves
And the percussion of wind riding through that tall
bamboo grove?
What clouds may appear and awaken her dread of
future fears?
Would this playful rattle now
Rear its head in a martial or meditative spear?
The dribble from his lips now from a nourishing feed
Could turn to cold blood as he lay
In permanent sleep on a distant battlefield.

For now this ocean of rest is deep
Even the poets cannot fill this child's ears with blessings
The way her love knows beyond sense and sound . . .

And it wasn't quite the way it had flashed in his mind's eye. So he closed his eyes and tried to concentrate on the seed of what the phrase was trying to say. He didn't want to analyse it or question it. Just live it—a mother would wish her child innocence. The sleep that comes with it visits only a child. A mother would do anything to shield her child from even the thought of danger . . . and with each word he slipped into a world of images accompanied by the sound of ocean waves so he could see clearer with his inner eye. He caught every hue, tone and colour of the sensation of a child's sleep, its quality watched by a mother. He heard the music in the sigh from the mother's breast and opened his eyes, driven to write the composition.

Instantly his enthusiasm left him. He froze. He rubbed his eyes. What was the dream? The mother's sigh in his musings or what he was confronting just now? Valmiki slapped his face and pulled his beard. He was awake. His blood was warm. He stared again. Lava was not lying asleep. *He was not there.* He was not anywhere. The sun had shifted. Was it really that long that Valmiki had been 'away'? 'If a blink of Brahma is an eon of time,' he thought with a great sense of futility. 'Aiyiyo, Narayana! What good is my knowledge, realization, composition . . .' he began to scold himself loudly. 'Here was a child created by man and woman, in flesh and blood. Its mother placed the child in my care. I put it there and was playing with it and now it's missing from under my very own nose! Maybe I shouldn't call Lava "it"!'

He was close to tears, he felt so helpless. He couldn't help thinking how all this was going to affect Sita. 'What all I have put her through in the Ramayana. Firstly, I did not give her an ordinary birth, so that she would be extra-ordinarily human. The one joy I gave her was Rama and their love. But before she could enjoy the privacy of her home, she accompanied Rama into exile. Then there was that abduction—how strong she was to have withstood the wiles of Ravana. At last Hanuman brought her comfort, and then . . . oh! Why is fiction truer than life? The humiliation of the fire test! That too she endured and was by then willing to leave the stage of private acts and public men. But I needed Sita to return to Ayodhya with Rama for the long-awaited coronation. What would life be like in the ordinary court, I thought, after all the epic struggles? And then, without my even dreaming it Sita became pregnant, and then Rama, secretly, exiled her.

'She has stayed on with me because she feels she has nowhere else to go. While she's been here she has taken care of everything; the one thing she had asked me to do was to look after Lava and what do I do? Go into a spell of composing! Aiyiyo! Where did this child go? How could he wander off when he was asleep? Which wild and stealthy creature has taken this child off for its meal? What a curse my intense concentration can be! That's why they called me *Valmiki*—the one who cannot be shaken—such that even an anthill has grown on top of him while he is lost in meditation. What good are these titles when a life is lost, and another life will be dead while living?'

He berated himself because he did not have the courage to see if there were signs of Lava being dragged away or, indeed, having been mutilated. How strange that his life as a ferocious highwayman and murderer, before he came to tell and write Ramayana, had completely washed away from him. For that he was ever thankful. The eternity of the imagination, the power of words, the meeting with Narada who had touched his soul. But what should he do now?

Words. Their power. It struck him. Another epiphany. He sat under a banyan tree. He sat on a deerskin. At an arm's length was the sacred kusa grass that had enabled many a disciple to enter deeper channels of meditation. This was the defining moment. Valmiki the creator distilled his humility, his intention to alleviate the burden of Sita's sorrow and the power of his imagination that he believed was a heightened truth. He stretched out his arm and plucked a single blade of kusa grass. Closing his eyes, he touched the wellspring of his knowledge and love. In the illumined lotus of his spirit centre he saw a steady flame shining. As his inner sight grew sharper he saw a male child who looked like Lava. 'Lava,' he said out loud. When he opened his eyes there was Lava.

Only, it was not Lava. It was an avatar of Lava created by Valmiki's imagination. Valmiki was enthralled. He realized how women felt when they gave birth and beheld their creation. He chuckled and started to play with this wonderful creation. And the creation responded as any lively child would.

'Maharaj! Maharaj!' It was Sita calling out. 'Please help me, I cannot carry this bundle as well.' And when Valmiki looked in the direction of the voice, Sita was standing with the bundle on the ground, and coiling her hair into a knot with Lava pulling her by her hand.

Sita and Valmiki looked at each other, then at Lava and the child beside Valmiki. Both were astounded. The two boys began to play. Valmiki leapt towards Lava and hugged him. 'Where did you vanish, my little one! I was so worried about you. I thought a tiger may have come and taken you away. I'm so happy you are safe.' Lava giggled as Valmiki's thick, knotted beard tickled him.

'But whose child is this?' inquired Sita who was by turns enchanted, surprised and intrigued at the resemblance to Lava.

Valmiki must have been in a parallel universe of reality following the tribulations of being an author before Sita arrived on the scene at the hermitage. 'Who? Oh, that! Him? Oh yes! Sita, what can I say . . .' and he began to tell her. 'But now that Lava is here, I can send him back into nothingness,' said Valmiki hesitantly, attempting to be conclusive. 'Into nothingness? Just like that? What is this, Maharaj? A game? Is life just a toy for some inventor? Now that you have created him he must stay. And we must hear his voice, just as he will become part of our story.' Valmiki could hear in Sita's voice genuine anguish at the notion of any kind of power over life—real or imagined.

A piercing squeal interrupted Valmiki and Sita's musings. Lava had gripped his new playmate's thigh with one hand and was in a wrestler's lock. The playmate squelched a handful of Lava's buttock and cried out, 'Koossa!' Lava let go his grip. He too let go and they rolled and tumbled and laughed. Sita repeated with great delight: 'Lava and Kusa!'

Mandodari

Valmiki now spent time being a little more alert to the things around him. With Lava and Kusa there were multiple questions that had to be answered instantly. Valmiki, as a poet, saw the boys as phrases, sounds, sentences budding from an image and slowly he started to see them as Sita did. Here were two young boys, in flesh and blood, who unravelled life's potential in every passing moment. If Lava was more interested in following Valmiki around and capturing sounds and exercising his lung power in reciting the improvised slokas, then Kusa would stay close to the women, using his tiny hands to be initiated into making herbal paste and sniffing the combination of ingredients. Kusa delighted in squelching and combining many unguents to daub himself. His various stages of anointment were received with Urmilla's 'Aeyee! That was meant for dry and wrinkled skin!' or 'No, no, that's not to be eaten, it's for healing eye infections!' and concluded with washing and drying, accompanied by hugs and a chorus of endearments. He had a tactility that Sita found herself being drawn towards, even if he was not her own flesh and blood.

One day Lava was out with Valmiki and Urmilla to learn how to make handheld catapults to knock guavas down from very high branches as the parrots had ravaged the fruit on the lower ones. Sita was in the kitchen. She had carefully swept with her hands the dry lentils that had spilled on the mud floor when she was measuring them to cook dal. She was on her haunches and was flicking a few lentils from her fingernails when Kusa, who was playing with the chapatti dough, asked, 'Amma, how were you born?' Sita blinked. 'Of course, yesterday was the boy's birthday, celebrated together with Lava's.' Sita had told them the story of how they were born, being economical with the truth as Lava and Kusa had come to regard themselves as identical and inseparable twins. While they looked identical, their emerging personalities emphasized different aspects of longing and fulfilment, endurance and resourcefulness that were also known to be strong aspects of Sita.

As she was wondering how to answer Kusa, so many memories came tumbling back to her that she could not make out which were real and which imagined. But within the shafts of the images she remembered, within each one of them, she realized there was a story that had to be told, and a story that had to be handed down to the boys as a chronicle of their origins. What was the story that she remembered about herself that she could tell Kusa? What was the story she would want to be remembered by?

She could feel herself squeeze through that narrow doorway of the past into another time. She screwed up her eyes as if to see clearly in the haze of the half-light. A woman stood in the doorway. When the woman turned, her diamond earrings and nose studs flashed like suns against her dark skin. The gold threads from her pomegranate-pink silk sari gleamed like the sun's reflection on a rippling river. Her voice was deep and bellyful and resonated from her nose. It was Mandodari. Ravana's queen and wife. For quite a while Sita sat, forgetting herself as she watched Mandodari tell Kusa a story.

'A long time ago a holy but poor man lived in a little thatched hut on an abandoned field. He used to wake every morning and bathe in a pond and pray to Vishnu, the great sustainer of life. Many people used to come to sit by him during the day and through his silence he was able to heal their family troubles. Vishnu, too, saw that this man did not crave anything in life except to help others. "How would he go about getting his food?" thought Vishnu, and decided that instead of the man having to go and seek alms or work to earn money, why not gift him a cow. Not just an ordinary cow but a holy cow. The man could carry on his work, and whether the cow went out to graze or not, it would give him a limitless supply of milk. The man collected the milk in a pot and sometimes he shared it with those who came to him to be healed. The poor man knew that this gift could have come only from Vishnu. So, as he thanked Vishnu while praying, he suddenly thought of Vishnu's wife Lakshmi, and hoped she would be born on earth as someone's daughter.

'At that very moment, he saw the clouds burst with a *Twaannngh!* in the sky. He could not see, but it was Ravana storming through the sky in his aerial chariot.

'Ravana was on a mission of "blood collecting" from holy men. This was a game, at first designed for his amusement. The rule was to seek out and spy on people who were considered holy. Then, with beguiling charm, Ravana would take on different disguises to question these people at a solitary moment about the nature of "Good". He had stunningly complex arguments. What was the need to be good or ethical? Why were a conscience and ethics always associated with "good"? What if we did not want to be good? Why did we have to have a sense of judgement? If life was about celebrating, why were there so many morals to keep us chained like prisoners when we could be free? If someone committed a wrong and fled the place, could anyone catch up with him? What on earth was a conscience? Why have one if it made you doubt everything you did? Why should one respect women? Weren't they all the same—sisters, wives, daughters, etc.? Why should we look after people who were disabled or care for children? Weakness should be put down, and why should the experience of an elder, who had no physical strength left, be considered? What did they have to teach us about life—nothing but regret.

'He defeated his opponents with well-illustrated and subtle arguments against good in human nature. He got a buzz in playing this game, and winning. Of course, he was always in disguise as a vulnerable contender, so he caught people unawares. But when a few people challenged him about the need to question one's actions and take responsibility for those actions, it stopped being a game. There was no buzz for Ravana when he wasn't winning. He soon discovered that one way of accounting for his successes was by collecting the blood of anyone who contested him, and labelling it "holy". The blood was preserved in several pots in his palace.

'On one such occasion, while he was lurking around the hut of the man with the holy cow—who had gone to the pond for his bath and prayers—Ravana found the pot of freshly drawn holy milk and stole it. Just for the sake of creating chaos.

'Ravana returned triumphant to his palace with the stolen pot. Then he mixed the blood from his other pots into it. Ravana called me, his queen, Mandodari, to hide the pot with the mixture of blood and milk (that had by now turned pink), and warned me that it contained poison. I knew the game he had begun to play had now turned into something exceedingly sinister.

'When Ravana left on yet another mission, I discovered through my secret intelligence services what he had done. I was disgusted by this behaviour. It made me wonder—why was I such a prisoner to all the silks, jewellery, feasts, slaves, servants, palaces and much more? Ravana had said he provided me with these to prove how well he looked after me, and how powerful his wealth made me. I was very proud to be his queen. But his power had gone so much to his head he could not see sense. I felt smaller than an ant that could be crushed under his foot. I was like anyone else in his life—he would tease and tease and tease till your heart and mind would explode. He was in total control. The way a frog is held in a snake's jaws—neither dead nor with the hope of life—just dying.

'When I learnt about the *blood collecting* of the holy men who had challenged his arguments, I wondered what would become of me? I was a mere woman, his wife—I could disappear and no one would know what really happened to me or be able to tell my story.

'He had gone away from the palace for some months to test a new range of deadly weapons. I prayed in secret. I prayed and prayed that someone should teach him such a lesson that—if he lived—he would never forget.

'As the days passed I grew afraid that there was nothing in the world that could defeat him; when even the gods were afraid, what chance did any animal or human have?

'Then it struck me like a thunderbolt! I prayed that a goddess be born on earth as a woman, and that she should defeat him. I prayed on behalf of all womankind.

'By now, I was so disgusted by the thoughts I was thinking, I wanted to finish myself. So I drank the blood mixture. Nothing happened.

'Meanwhile, I think the wishes of the holy man, who had prayed that Lakshmi be born on earth, came true. I heard, across the ocean, in the kingdom of Mithila, King Janaka was ploughing a field. He saw something glistening in the distance. As he approached the spot he noticed a crystal cradle that was wedged between the furrows of the earth, and there was a baby girl in it. She looked radiant.

He held the child close to his face as if she were an answer to a long-forgotten prayer and took her home to his queen. As she was found in the furrows of the earth, the child was named Sita.

'All this happened in the flash of an instant when Lakshmi vanished from Devaloka, when Narada cursed the maid of honour, when there was a *Twaannngh* that sounded like it came from a cloudburst. Lakshmi had fulfilled a poor holy man's prayer that she be born as a human on earth. The devas, viewing this sight from Devaloka, sighed with relief.

'The following years I sent out various spirits and spies to feed me with the hope that such a woman had indeed been born. They gave me news and I found hope.'

Sita was loved dearly by her royal parents. As she was an only child, Urmilla was adopted as her sister. Sita was quick to make friends, and she treated them as her equals. She would have bouts of fiery temper, especially if someone had been deceitful. But she had a quick wit, a sense of humour that endeared her to everyone because she could bend any sorrow with a lightness of word or touch, without being insensitive or careless. Her nature was fed by fire. She had an unquenchable desire to live, and celebrate life in all its tints and hues.

King Janaka had a prosperous kingdom that rivalled Dasaratha's. But it was not as vast as Kosala, which had a natural gift of three rivers flowing around it, making it extremely fertile. Mithila depended on trade with other kingdoms and also knew the significance of strong regional relationships, rather than standing apart in isolation. This enabled the citizens of Mithila to feel safe. A healthy economy and a sense of security often make people feel they can take time out on holidays, or spend time planning elaborate rituals, like naming ceremonies for babies, ceremonies on becoming a teenager, or just travelling and enjoying the countryside away from life in court.

Janaka insisted on holidays for three reasons. Firstly, it connected people who lived and worked at court to experience the pace of rural life; secondly, it enabled courtiers to discover the requirements of villagers in an unofficial capacity. The third reason was that while on holiday, one could plan for the future. For Janaka, holidays helped him think clearly, away from the pressures of a daily schedule of meetings. It was sheer joy being in the company of his wife, his daughter, Sita, and their friends.

Janaka had an orchard with fruit trees at the back of the holiday resort palace. He kept a limited number of servants there; this enabled him to be himself and prepare for his final ashrama, that is, retirement, when he would have to do the daily chores himself.

He would pray to Shiva with a sincere heart, every day without fail. One afternoon he noticed a giant iron bow half buried in the earth, standing up to the height of a banana tree! It was inscribed: 'Janaka, a gift of love—Shiva.'

'What in heaven's name was the use for a bow, that too this size, in a vegetable garden when one was on holiday! For Karma's sake,' thought Janaka, 'I have no intention, inclination or time to show any neighbouring kingdom how mighty Mithila is!'

As it was hidden amidst the banana trees, he decided to leave the bow there while he went away and thought about the best way to show his gratitude to Shiva. He did not want to endanger his kingdom by revealing to Mithila's neighbours the huge iron bow and what it could signal: capability of war.

His queen had cooked him a simple and satisfying meal. Just as Janaka finished and went to the inner courtyard to wash his hands and rinse his mouth, he could see straight through the doorway. What did he see? Sita looking up at the bow. She was in one of her clearing-up-the-garden moods. She had her arms akimbo and her head tilted to fathom the actual size of the bow underground from its height above ground. Then in a flash, Janaka saw his fifteen-year-old Sita lunge for the bow at its widest arc and, with both her hands, pull it out and fling it away. 'Yes! Take that!' she shouted gleefully, dusting her hands matter-of-factly. 'That'll teach you to wedge into the roots of these fruit trees! What a mess this is.' And she began levelling the yawning hole in the ground with the rubble around it.

Janaka was awestruck. That was Shiva's bow Sita had just plucked out and chucked like some soft, rotting plant! Throughout lunch he had been calculating how many men he would have to get to dig that bow out of the ground to then heave it on to a chariot and carry it back to Mithila. 'Oh, it doesn't bear thinking,' he said to himself. Then something dawned on him. 'Sita! Even she is not aware how extraordinary she is.' That beam of light in her eyes, the fire in her soul, were all signs of how blessed he and his wife were to have her as their daughter. He thought it best not to say anything either to his wife or to Urmilla.

Two weeks passed. Spring was in the air and bullock horns were painted with vermilion and turmeric, strung with flowers, bells and streamers. It was time to return to court for the royal festivities marking the birth of a new season.

Janaka, his wife and Sita, with her favourite Urmilla, were returning in the royal chariot. They were often accompanied by the female storyteller who knew a thing or two about the different villages and towns they passed en route to Mithila. Somehow, she always got wind of the latest news, and this was Janaka's best way of keeping up with what had happened while he had been away from court.

A female storyteller never just reports facts; she adds wonderful emotional twists and turns to events, and gives insightful details about the people she meets. Urmilla and Sita were listening to the latest news about two young men from the Kosala kingdom who had entered the Dandaka forest accompanied by Vishwamitra. 'Do you know what they saw?' The storyteller's eyes widened as she could see it clearly in her mind's eye. 'They came upon a large, black rock. One of the young men, being curious as young men are, was examining this strange stone. His toe grazed its base. And, suddenly, it burst into a soft flame, and a woman emerged from it. Her name was Ahalya. She was so radiant, had always been a real beauty. You know what her name means?' Without waiting for a response from the royals, she continued, 'The one in whom there is no imperfection.'

'I cannot even imagine it,' said Urmilla excitedly.

'You mean it is even greater than being just perfect?' demanded Sita indignantly.

'Now that's something for you two to live up to,' said the queen with a warm laugh.

'So, what happened?' asked Janaka, as he wanted to find out about the two young men, while masking his concern for his kingdom's safety.

The storyteller continued cheerfully, impervious to these lively interruptions:

'It was long before my mother's, mother's grandmother's great aunt's time that if any woman's beauty was compared to Ahalya's, all the neighbours would "tut, tut". It wasn't just her beauty, it was her nature that was beyond comparison.

'She was a caring woman. She loved her husband who was many, many, many years older than her. He was a great philosopher of his time. There they both were, in the forest, in a little hermitage. He used to wake early and go off to meditate and she would make the place spotless by the time he returned.

'When the devas watched over the couple, they couldn't help wondering what it would be like to be close to her. Finally Indra, the chieftain of the devas, could hold back no longer. He thought of Ahalya night and day, and day and night. All the courtesans of Devaloka grew ferociously jealous of an earthly woman holding sway over a deva, and that too over Indra. They taunted him. He found this a good excuse to come down to earth and prove what a powerful deva he really was; that no one could stand in the way of such striking godliness. But as the deva who held the thunderbolt and struck lightning, he decided not to descend to earth so dramatically. It would scare everyone off. He knew the only way he could come into Ahalya's presence was if he were someone else.

'So, Indra waited for the husband to leave the hermitage. Then, transforming himself into the husband's double, Indra approached Ahalya. Well . . . Indra seized the moment when Ahalya was alone. She had never felt the kind of desire that swept through her like a forest fire. For the first time she sensed something other than the desire to serve. It rushed through her body to see her husband, standing before her, seducing her. And so . . . she gave herself as she took him like the current of a river speeds the course of a boat. The current was swift and raging, and the banks along the river dissolved into the water. Ahalya had never thought of love. The joy of being, desire, being desired, giving and taking had unravelled for her the secrets of the dark of a woman's body. And then, her husband returned to the hermitage to fetch the jar of water that he had left behind. He saw the couple in the throes of pleasure . . .'

'Then what happened?' asked the queen, genuinely startled by the turn of events in the story.

'When Ahalya's husband appeared, however great a sage or thinker he may have been, reflecting on grand things like immortality, the nature of life and death . . .'

'Go on, go on,' urged Janaka.

'He cursed both his wife and Indra. Ahalya was shocked both at being deceived and "discovered" and she protested. But her husband would have none of it. In response to her protests, her husband uttered a curse. She turned to stone and remained that way for many, many, many years. Her husband did add a condition, though, even to the everlasting curse. That in the future, a man who was fair and sympathetic to the unjustly accused and who saw only the good in others would pass by. When he would touch the stone, the spell would be broken and she would be free.'

'And such a man entered Dandaka just a few days ago?' asked Sita, amazed.

'Not only that, Your Highness,' said the chariot driver, 'he has also put an end to the terror in the forests by doing away with the wretched rakshasas, Tataka and Subahu.'

'Wonder of wonders!' said Janaka; Sita added, rather thoughtfully: 'And you say such a man is on his way?'

Soorpanakka

Lava, Urmilla and Valmiki had now fashioned the perfect handheld catapult. Urmilla had collected the gut strings from carcasses in the forest on her earlier expeditions in search of herbs for her ointments. She had created a strap that enabled the catapult to be elastic enough for Lava's small hands. Standing behind him, she held his hand, which encircled a large reetha soap nut, with the gut string firmly wound around his left thumb and index finger. The right pulled and released the reetha soap nut into space with sufficient force, so that by its volition it struck the guava dangling from the top branch. It hit the ground with a soft thud as the parrots fluttered out in a trail, shrieking. It was Lava's first conquest. He jumped with glee. 'My, what a marksman you are, Lava! Be careful what you aim for,' Urmilla said, bursting with pride.

'So, Lava, full marks on the aim, timing, focusing on target and concentration. What we travelled across was distance. That was a fruit. Tomorrow it could be an animal. All these have life.' What Valmiki wanted to add was 'and one day it will be your own thought that will propel your action; so heed your intention, dear Lava, as the world will depend on it', but the epic poet in him couldn't brave being so prosaic at a moment of such triumph in Lava's animated life.

Lava's face furrowed. 'What do you mean? We need to eat, and they are there for us,' he said with indignant authority.

'Spoken like a king, my dear, mm . . . but not a wise and loving one,' said Urmilla, reading Valmiki's disapproval.

'Yes, but consider that the fruit, birds, all creatures, this earth too, are generous in giving—consciously or unconsciously. Let me tell you a story. When I've finished, I want you to tell me what you can see inside your mind's eye as you are listening to it. Okay?' Lava was all ears with his chin cupped in his hands. He had stretched out, lying on his stomach on the cool forest floor, gazing up at Valmiki who had entered the galaxy of his story. The words from Valmiki's voice flowed like a mist encircling his audience of Lava, Urmilla and the inhabitants of the entire forest, from the minutest algae to the mightiest carnivores.

The afternoon heat began to dissolve as his voice took on an even timbre, harmonizing with the sound of the rippling forest stream. But at any relevant moment within the story, Valmiki could leap out of his skin with the force of a tiger to ask a question about the here and now.

'It was a time of change. Change never happens suddenly, although it may seem so. Like a rock chipping away from a boulder, hurtling towards a rapid river.

'Sage Rishyasringa could see the flames from the altar rising like a winged messenger from the belly of the earth to the sky. At the auspicious hour of the ritual it was still dark. It had to be, because the time that the gods watch over the world is 4 a.m. It is also the hour of our deepest rest when the imagination and gods are at play. The sage could see the flames like a cord of hope rising from human prayers to the gods in the heavens. At that very moment the devas, or "shining ones", were having a conference and had gathered outside Brahma's Assembly Hall. Devaloka is made up of gods, or shining ones, and above them are the mahadevas, whom I call the Greats—they are Brahma, Vishnu and Shiva. At the time of the Ashwamedha, as Rishyasringa watched the flames from the altar on earth reaching the heavens, or Vaikunta, Vishnu was in a highly confidential discussion with Brahma. A new situation had been created that was to spell the fate of the world.

'After the Big Bang and the creation of the universe, there was a time of famine and drought brought on by neglect. Some of the gods turned into ferocious and ever-hungry creatures that became ogres, monsters and demons known as asuras. In time, Ravana, the descendent of an ogre, conquered all the other asuras. He then prayed fervently to Shiva for a vardana, or boon. It was not a simple prayer of bending on a knee with folded hands and making a special wish. Ravana had to do something spectacular. Only he could; he was strong, skilful and brave and also deeply misunderstood, which made him very lonely. He loved being noticed. So, he hung upside down from a tree over a fire and thought of nothing and no one except Shiva for forty years. He wasn't noticed. He decided to climb down and see what he could do for the gods who were a little worried about crossing the bridge of Devaloka into the human world, as a serpent was threatening them. The gods didn't want to get their hands, silks, crowns and jewels dirty, so Ravana decided to help them and killed the serpent. Finally, he had a vision of Shiva. Shiva the Great was delighted by his penance and asked him what his wish was. Ravana replied, "I wish for immortality. You know what I mean. Life, forever and beyond ever!"

'Shiva simply said: "Sorry, most-competent-of-all Asura, but you cannot have it. It is reserved. Your labours and devotion to seek my attention are seriously impressive. So, sorry. Some *can* have life everlasting, but unfortunately you are not born to."

'Ravana would not return disappointed. He huffed and he puffed as he stamped down on the big smoky coils of his fury that were flying out like clouds of stinging mosquitoes. Then he asked the Great Shiva if he could be made invincible against the gods, so that none could injure or kill him. It seemed a fair deal. Shiva, always known for his generosity, was pleased with what seemed like Ravana's compromise and the wish was granted.

'Ravana was given the beautiful island of Lanka to rule over. He ruled well, became terrifyingly powerful and was a law unto himself. His arts of magic and cloning of the existing worlds began to trouble the gods. And, thanks to Shiva, no one, not even Indra, the chieftain of the devas and godfather of the heavens, could devise a strategy that would keep Ravana in check. The fate of the heavens was at stake because Ravana was beginning to invade peoples' minds with dreams and illusions of power in pursuit of personal gain harmful to others. This brought in its wake greed, conquest, discontent and a disregard for humanity. It was the reversal of aspiration, achievement and fulfilment—the profound ideals that are the essence of being human. This was why the devas had gathered outside Brahma's Assembly Hall; they wanted to know what was the antidote to Shiva's boon of near immortality that had been granted to Ravana.

'Down on earth, Rishyasringa was placing sacred barks and twigs with pure ghee as oblation on the ritual fire, while in Devaloka, Brahma waited breathlessly for Vishnu's decision.

'But Vishnu smiled charmingly as he said, "You mean . . . Ravana is causing all this . . . by himself?"

'Brahma was embarrassed. He coughed slightly. On earth, it caused rolling thunder in the sky. He knew what Vishnu was implying. What were the devas doing, indulging in all the luxuries of heaven, enjoying immortality and neglecting people, while one asura had such amazing powers to destroy the universe? Brahma admitted to himself that it was time he made cuts on some executive privileges and extravagant personal expenses of the devas. "Well . . . er, hmmm . . ." was all he could say. On earth everyone felt an earthquake.

'Shiva had just entered the Great Assembly Hall. He was frowning. Nandi, his wise old bull who accompanied him everywhere, was fidgety and whisked his tail. It got entangled in Shiva's cascading locks of hair. "How many times do I have to tell you not to do that?" Shiva said to Nandi. "Well, I think it's time you had a haircut and I think it's time you took some responsibility for all the mess the world is in!" was Nandi's sharp reply.

'"Order! Order!" said Brahma. "What does it look like? The devas are waiting for us to do something about Creation, Dasaratha is holding a yagna sacrifice calling on the gods to give him and his three wives children, and we are behaving like urchins fighting in the gutter over a tired allegation like a bone spat out by a dog!"

'"Are you all blaming *me*?" asked Shiva, genuinely perplexed, and glared at Nandi. "I had nothing to do with it. Ravana worked very hard at contacting me. Not only that, he showed such promise. He's bright, hands-on and doesn't leave the hard work for others to do. He has spectacular ideas and he knows how to make them happen."

'"But surely," Nandi cut in, "you must screen *who* you grant boons to and give some thought to what *kind* of boons you grant?"

'Vishnu was listening and, with his mischievous crooked smile, said, "I remember how Ravana taunted me in the last encounter." "Yes," Shiva said eagerly, having found an ally, "that's right Vishnu, you tell them. When Ravana was in the form of Nandaka and got a little out of hand about the immortality business, I did try to burn him with my third eye, didn't I? Just tell them."

'"Yes," said Nandi a little cheekily, "you're so generous about keeping your promises—you gave him a diamond finger so he could kill anything and anyone just by pointing it at them."

"'He threatened everyone, even the gods," said Brahma and continued, "Thank goodness, Vishnu had the good sense to enchant him in the guise of a female dancer and . . .'"

"'Yes, that was sooper!" said Shiva, who is also the creator of dance, "You got him to copy all your movements and then pointed your finger to your thigh and when he did the same . . . Ba-buh-bah-Booommm! He exploded!" They all laughed uproariously. The thunder rolled, lightning struck and the wind howled as if with laughter.

'On earth, Rishyasringa, dipped the sacred kusa grass in the loshta vessel, and raised it to the heavens in an urgent prayer for divine intervention. The sacred flames grew higher.

'Brahma, Vishnu and Shiva could feel the amber glow of its warmth. The laughter subsided. Vishnu said, "It is time. When I destroyed Ravana the last time, he mocked me saying I had deceived him as a woman and it wasn't fair. Now I must fight him as a man."

'Nandi sighed.

"'I will be born as Dasaratha's son," said Vishnu decisively and smiled.

'Brahma and Shiva embraced their friend and, speaking as one, said, "You will forget where you have come from.

You will fight with the heart and mind of a man. Our energy is always there for you to draw from. It will help you triumph. But do not forget that every cell of creation, every atom of being, is light. Keep truth and love as your weapons against the dark forces of delusion. That will make everything return to light, where everything belongs. Remember, you are not alone."

'Some of the brighter devas who had gathered outside were able to tune into the frequency of the airwaves in which Brahma and Shiva were speaking. They led the chorus in Devaloka: "*Truth Will Triumph with Light; No More Delusion and Darkness . . . Truth Will Triumph with Light!*"

'On earth the wind stopped howling. Everyone looked up. The clouds were clearing and a soft amethyst glow spread across the sky. There was a light shower of rain and then the warm, moist air filled with a scattering of fragrant kannakambaram and mallika petals and tulasi leaves. "Very auspicious signs, a good omen!" the crowds of Ayodhya murmured.

'In Ayodhya, the eagle-shaped enclosure reserved for royal religious ceremonies was studded with rubies and emeralds encased in gold. King Dasaratha sat inside it, with his three wives seated on each side of the square fire altar. Agni was the fire deva creating a bridge with his golden cord of flames between earth and Devaloka. Agni in the form of pure fire was always called upon to translate people's prayers to the Greats and be the bridge between human longing and its fulfilment.

'Dasaratha had been listening to all the sacred and purifying chants with concentration. When it was time to offer his personal prayers, he washed his hands with the gulak water and folded his palms. Eyes closed, he prayed with intense longing, and love, for a son and an heir.

'More sacred herbs, roots and fragmented barks of tree were delicately cast into the sacrificial fire. The golden flames began to rise gently at first and then to leap. In the midst of it, a golden figure appeared. Through the veil of fire it looked at first like a golden lion sitting on its haunches. The flames and the fur were of the same burnished gold. It roared within the blazing fire. As the lion seemed to descend from the sky like a chariot of the devas within the diminishing flames, it turned into a goddess. She was dressed in gold with blood-red and dark blue gems glistening about her neck, wrists, ears, head and feet. She held a golden bowl with a carved lid. It was an awesome sight. Dasaratha was dazed and speechless. He stood with hands outstretched to salute the goddess; instead, he found he was holding the golden bowl. It was not a figment of his imagination! When he looked again, the goddess had vanished and the golden flames were dancing, kissing and crackling.

'As he held the precious bowl, he looked at Rishyasringa. Dasaratha did not want to do anything that would interfere or disrespect the ritual. He was visibly trembling with excitement when he was signalled to open it. It was payasam, the food of the gods. It tasted like the nectar of goodness. He offered a ladle of it to his first wife, Kausalya. She tasted it, thinking "Ummm . . ." and, with great dignity, ate the payasam. He then gave another ladleful to Queen Sumitra, his second wife—"Umm . . . this is out of the world," she couldn't help thinking and wanted more, but Dasaratha was by then offering a ladle of the payasam to Queen Kaikeyi, his luscious third wife. Dasaratha could not resist the look in Queen Sumitra's twinkling eyes and decided to give her what was remaining in the vessel. A few more ceremonies were conducted till the sun emerged like a vermilion dot on the forehead of the sky. The ritual would be embedded in the memory of everyone in Kosala for generations to come. The bridge of longing had been crossed; the king and his queens had arrived on the banks of their fulfilment.

'A few moments ago the Greats were having their exclusive meeting that resulted in Vishnu going down to earth. Just outside the Great Assembly Hall, the Great Wives—Saraswati, Lakshmi and Parvati—were at the gathering of the gods. Brahma loved his Saraswati for her wide knowledge, the rhythmical and clear words she chose to define things, beings and situations. Here she was, listening to the devas and their suffering as a result of Ravana's masquerades. She was placing their grievances in categories, creating arguments and labelling them with observations so that if a trial were to be held, there would be a source of evidence of the crimes. In another part of the gathering, some goddesses were insinuating and Parvati was defending her Shiva. She was holding on to Ganesha, her son, so that he wouldn't get lost among the crowd of adult devas. He was busy rubbing his trunk and his belly. The devas were always careful when they spoke to Parvati. She had rather extreme means of sorting out nuisances. Without a doubt, she was loved by all as a benign mother of humanity. But in a flash she could turn into Kali, a ferocious mother, if she perceived any threat to Creation. She was reputed for matching a vicious asura in terror and strength and finally killing him.

'Ganesha suddenly saw his favourite aunt, goddess Lakshmi. He waddled speedily to her side as she was offering a tray of heavenly laddoos latticed with cardamom, roasted cashew nuts, ghee and honey. Lakshmi had brought these back from the yearly ocean-of-consciousness holiday that she and Vishnu had just been on. Ganesha took her blessings and began to pick and eat the laddoos with the speed and skill of a juggling dancer, bringing merriment to the gathering. Lakshmi was comforting those who had lost their health and wealth at the hands of Ravana. She admired the humility and courage that some of these devas showed in wanting to go down to earth as humans, animals, mountains, herbs, in short anything, to restore safety and happiness to the world. But everyone was waiting to hear the decision of the Greats.

'Suddenly there was a big *Twaannngh!* It sounded like the plucking of a string of a gigantic musical instrument. Everyone whirled around. A woman, one of Lakshmi's maids of honour, came running in, wailing and spluttering, "How could he! Oh, whose face did I see this morning that such bad tidings should be heard! Please, all you devas and devis, forgive me. I was only doing my duty to my goddess Lakshmi by keeping trespassers out. And now, this . . . the curse . . . what will we ever do . . ." and on and on she wailed. Everyone whirled around again to see Lakshmi's reaction. But she wasn't there. She had vanished.

'On earth, in Ayodhya and all across the kingdoms of Kosala, people talked for months on end about the Ashwamedha that proclaimed Dasaratha King of Kings and about the fire sacrifice to the devas. At the end of nine months there was another grand celebration to top the earlier one. Dasaratha's three wives gave birth to four sons. Kausalya gave birth to Rama; Sumitra, who had twins, gave birth to Lakshmana and Shatrughana; and Kaikeyi gave birth to Bharata.

'Just as we live here, there are other beings among us whom we cannot always see. They are not up there or down here or below us, but sometimes we imagine they are. They enter our lives, they are real and they challenge us and our convictions. It's a game, but it is also real. Finally, we have to work towards forgetting our little selves, while protecting what is discovered as the secret to our happiness. The great test is in finding a way that ushers in everyone else's well-being and also gives us happiness.

'Imagine that!'

Valmiki paused. Urmilla and Lava were enraptured by the story, each taking it at their level of comprehension. They were completely unaware that someone was watching, waiting and listening.

It was none other than Soorpanakka. She was Ravana's sister. After his death she roamed across the earth, not exactly mourning but seeing how people and values evolved after her brother's passing. As she happened to hear Valmiki mention Ravana in his story, she was attracted by the power of her brother's name and swiftly inhabited a tree. Valmiki could sense a change in the atmosphere as a spirit now occupied a tree not far behind him, so he chanted a mantra:

May we who listen to stories that enchant our minds
Be ever wakeful to the shining, the glorious, the Lotus-Eyed

Within us;
That It may shine undimmed.
Across all the hills, forests, valleys and plains that our
eyes can see
May our hearts unfold the journey within.
May the ever-revolving disc of consciousness splinter
darkness with light
May words flow into the sound of the conch shell
That emerges from the embryo of our being
Defining space around us and within us to live in
peace.
Shantih, shantih shantih

It seemed to cast a spell like a veil around the tree that Soorpanakka had inhabited. Entranced by his words, she began to remember, and paused to reflect on her own encounter with Sita.

'Life didn't really begin before noon for us rakshasas. The humidity and heat would make all those early risers seek the shade. We would dwell by wells and hover around the tamarind trees that were laden with teeth-sharpening sour fruit. The night was our time for entertainment and revelry. On one such night we heard news about a dim and distant place far north from ours, where a swayamvara was being held. Our customs were different. Quite often, we rakshasa females had to seek the male, and that gave us freedom. I, born of a royal rakshasa clan, always had the first choice. But I was curious to delve into the world of humans. And I knew that at a swayamvara there would be many men. More likely, young men who were not yet aware of how we rakshasas operated and the spells we could cast on them.

'So I arrived in Mithila, where this great assembly of princes from kingdoms far and near was to take place. I don't get impressed easily, because I am particular about my comforts. Some call it indulgence, luxury, whatever! But I have a high standard that must be maintained. And in Mithila I was impressed. It's a pity the bedsteads weren't covered with gold and precious jewels, but at least it had brocade awnings and there were many late-night distractions. I normally like to visit gambling dens—that's where men are most vulnerable—and brothels are the best place to get the real gossip about the politics of the state. That's where you will find the police and the politicians divulging state secrets as they pour state money into their leisure, which they call "privileges".

'In Mithila, the brothels seemed filled with courtiers and soldiers of the visiting princes. The princes were in their guesthouses getting ready for the great contest the next day. "How absurd!" I thought. Here's the time for the best stag night, because who knows how marriage can turn out, and all these young princes were wasting time praying and hoping that they be the chosen one. What was *so* special about the bride-to-be?

'I was having fun shifting my shape from a water carrier to a vegetable seller to the sugar cane juice supplier to a fish wife to a well-paid prostitute to the madam of a brothel so I could hear a range of news, add my little mischief, get people quarrelling and have fun watching them try to get out of those muddles. During my role as the madam, just as I was tucking a bag of coins into my bodice, there was a hue and cry in the street over a grand procession. It was my beloved brother Ravana arriving in the dead of the night. He was being carried on a grand palanquin; his chariot was too wide to fit the roads of Mithila. He always brought his own apartments, servants and courtiers and lived royally wherever he went. When he had settled down, I decided to go and dine with him, and so I did in a flash.

'"You're not serious about entering the 'competition', are you? You'll beat them black and blue, turn them inside out and leave them hollow! Why waste that energy? Surely you're above all these humans? Why not grab the prize and fly away?" I asked my brother frankly.

'He was sitting cross-legged, holding his right big toe with his left hand. For a moment his body seemed still. "This is a prize I want to win. It is boring not to have a challenge. I want this prize to be won over by me." That was all he said before he entered his inner apartments to take rest before the swayamvara.

'I couldn't understand what had come over him. It certainly wasn't because the prize was a woman. My sister-in-law Mandodari was no less. She had all the rakshasa dignity of staging a fight with artifice and accomplishment that the opponent would whimper away, begging her forgiveness. She was a great queen, but sometimes she was under the cloud of that curse that humans tend to have—self-reflection. She always felt torn and twisted when what the human civilization calls "conscience" churned within her. Later, she began to get bouts of trembling; her forehead would sweat profusely when she would hear the cats calling at night. She would often say, "Oh, why is that child not being fed with milk?" and make her maids of honour run out to see if there were children roaming in the dark. She felt a tenderness for baby rakshasas long after her son had grown up. Her crying really got Ravana upset. He had high regard for her, but the outbursts became frequent before the war. I wonder if she could see that she was going to be widowed.

'But back to this prize business. I was curious. So there I was, bright and early, at the contest. My word! You should have seen all those princes; their bare upper bodies glinting with all that jewellery and marked with sandal and vermilion. It was arousing to say the least.

'The city was festooned with banners carried by the entourage of the participating princes. All banners were embossed with images of the princes' guardian deities— some were embossed with a lion, some had an eagle, some an owl, another a cobra, yet another a peacock, and on and on it went as the procession stretched beyond a mile.

'Each entourage consisted of the princes' poets, masseurs, astrologists, musicians, councillors, palmists, poison detectives, historians, portrait painters, sartorial advisers and accompanying brahmins to invoke the respective gods of strength to win the contest. The people of Mithila had swept and washed the roads till they gleamed in the sun. Sugar cane juice in clay cups was offered as a welcome drink. Water carriers stood along the roadside ready to refresh any member of the entourage. There were elephant sheds and stables provided for each visiting principality. Food, drink and diverse entertainments were provided by the royal courtesy of Mithila. Perhaps at any other contest, a prince's entourage could stir a little trouble by drinking too much, losing at gambling or the cockfight, or because a dancing girl slapped them too hard. But here, on this occasion, the contest and where it was being held had a special significance.

'It was Mithila—a coveted city within a coveted kingdom. The princes had been waiting eagerly for the announcement of this swayamvara for months, even a year.

They had been training for longer. Each prince wanted to exhibit his skills and show his prowess. Nothing and nobody could cast a slur on that one ambition that filled each prince as he journeyed to Mithila. But why?

'Because each prince dreamed of winning the prize of the contest. The prize was Sita. Sita's wit and fiery spirit had caught the attention of poets and won the praise of singers when they had attended arts festivals at Mithila. They had created legends about her; and when they returned to their courts and sang, each prince grew to love Sita and wanted her as his wife.

'The whole of Mithila was bustling with guests and the streets hummed with languages of other kingdoms. The kitchens were steaming with cuisines for vegetarians and meat-eaters. Stalls were dressed with sweets of all colours and shapes, glistening with silver trimming, and the air was heavy with the subtle scents of condiments like green cardamom, clove, nutmeg and saffron mixing in sweetened, thickened cow's milk. Weavers spread out their bales of rich turquoise- and ruby-coloured silk. The stone cutters' chisels and hammers created early morning music as they carved out of soapstone and alabaster statuettes of women in all forms of movement, subliminally celebrating the vivacity of their princess Sita—not wishing to disclose her identity for fear of staining her fiery and pure spirit by replicating it in stone and wood. "How can we," the master craftsmen would cry with dismay and pride, "capture that spark that lights her eyes?"

'Sage Vishwamitra glided past the crowds with his two able adjutants who wore their hair long and tied in a topknot; I suppose it was because the aides travelled through difficult terrain where grooming could be time-consuming. They wore dhotis made of bark and carried a quiver of arrows slung on their backs. Their torsos were bare and they could well have been mistaken for forest folk. Other princes dared not sneer at them as they both had a stately presence—these were cultured and strong young men. To undermine their dignity would've been reckless and betrayed the other princes' crassness or anxiety. The eligibility to the swayamvara was on fair terms—anyone who had training and was recommended by an accredited brahmin or sportsman was welcome. Vishwamitra's adjutants were invited to the Mithila Assembly Hall.

'It was vast. A huge gong was struck and the waves of sound reverberated through the city. First the conch shell, a symbol of the presence of Vishnu, who inhabits sound and space, was blown. Everyone—princes, entourages, courtiers and invited commoners of Mithila—was hushed. Then the liveried trumpeters announced the powerful ministers into Mithila's court, then the brahmins, the sages, and finally King Janaka.

'Another gong sounded with several chimes, and a gold-embossed screen that looked like a wall parted in two. When it had slid open, a golden chariot covered with a sapphire-blue velvet drape emerged. The chariot moved on wheels guided by eight hundred footmen. It had been timed perfectly—swift enough not to bore the spectators and steady enough so that everyone marvelled at the feat of sliding a long chariot into the even larger Assembly Hall. Another flourish of string and percussion instruments, and trapeze artists flew in from their perches at the corners of the ceiling. With bows like Kama's, they shot hooked arrows at the edges of the drapes and pulled it up in unison in a fly-past dance. Everyone's mouth popped open, gasping at this synchronized act. Thunderous applause greeted the sight of the drape being carried away to reveal Shiva's giant iron bow.

'It seemed as if this was the moment everyone had been waiting for. The princes had not been allowed to even look at this monster of an object as they prepared themselves. Even I was staggered. I had shape-shifted into one of the dancers so I could have a good view of the eager princes. How unfortunate that they were all set on the same object for their prize! The bow was no ordinary bow. I quickly estimated its weight, scale and size. But it was more than that. With my exquisite fine-tuning barometer I could gauge a sound emitting from it that carried vibrations. Part of the preparations, I thought, must be to block its sound emissions. They just made your brain whirr. But here were these princes, each twirling his moustache or stroking his sideburns studded with gems. As the princes flexed their muscles and slapped their bare thighs, getting ready for their turn, the look in each man's eye, his show of power and his open sexual desire sent waves of excitement through my being. You could smell the sweat mixed with fear and courage, the fleeting scent of testosterone underneath the perfumed oils of jasmine, sandalwood, rose and musk.

'I remember the whirring from the bow became bearable to my ears when Vishwamitra strode in. I was watching everything but hadn't paid much attention to his adjutants. But now, as all the princes stood in their regalia, in walked these two youths dressed like forest folk. Had it not been for their radiance and royal bearing, they would have been smothered with ash and mistaken for ascetics. I suppose you could say that they attracted attention because they weren't really dressed for the occasion.

'It was time for the championships to begin. Four hundred and ninety-eight princes had decided to compete. It seemed an odd number. But, among them, Ravana had registered for two places as his entourage was twice as big as any other prince's, and he wanted to have two attempts at winning Sita as his prize. The great sages, who can see beyond the realm of the physical body, often drew him in their scrolls as having ten resplendent heads and twenty arms. He was very accomplished but his complexity and ego got the better of him, time after time.

'Vishwamitra stood on the sidelines with his two adjutants. Following the fanfare, the first prince was announced. Heralding him, his court singer chanted melodically, and rather pompously, about the ancestors of the prince and how worthy he was. The prince proceeded to climb five steps up to a platform where the entire gathering could see him. For the people in the city streets, a poet from the court stood on a stone above a secret passage that filtered the sound of what he recited. These proceedings were heard by the town crier at the end of the secret passage; facing the street directly, he reported the spectacle to the whole city and its visitors.

'As the princes came forward—some with braided hair, others with topiaried sideburns; some with waxed whiskers embroidered with precious gems, others with bejewelled tattoos—each one wanted the chronicles to record that in his youth he had attempted to win Sita by trying to lift that impossible bow. Having had the chance, not only did they return to the arms of their masseurs, collapsing like tents in a thunderstorm, but with broken backs and hearts.

'Ravana went forward. He, who had killed the serpent that had frightened the gods, now had his turn. The teeth of many princes chattered and their bones rattled; the earth trembled and juddered with each step that Ravana took towards the platform. Vishwamitra sighed. Ravana twirled his moustache. He was the only contestant in the swayamvara who was competing wearing his crown and his jewels. He stood with his left foot on a lower level as his right foot stepped higher. It was the stance of an indefatigable wrestler. He slapped his right thigh—*smack!* It resounded in the Assembly Hall like a thunderclap. He bent down to touch the bow. It felt like running water, so light through his fingers. When he tried to get a grip, it felt like the weight of the universe was pulling him into the ground. His masseurs tried to deceitfully web his feet to the ground so he would not slip, but Ravana snarled with viciousness and vowed to break their legs.

'Each contestant was given a specific time for his attempt at lifting the bow. Ravana had been distracted by his masseurs. Second attempt. He stretched his arms into the air and lunged to pick up the bow. The blood rushed to his head, and, as he let out the grunt and wail of weightlifters when he seized the bow, the channel of water that measured the time gong chimed loudly, setting off prisms of light so that the contestant had to stop. Phew! Ravana seemed almost relieved this ordeal was over. He would not, indeed he could not, lift that bow. Majestically, sneering at the timekeepers, he covered the wounds of his broken heart with a scornful smile that indicated the challenge was not sophisticated enough for the likes of him.

'He strode out of the Assembly Hall with what everyone else read as contempt. There was an uneasy silence. This was followed by the final, or the "499th", contestant. He was a wiry fellow with a dismissive manner that could reduce anything to nothing with his cynicism. When he saw that Ravana was defeated by the task, he knew what his fate would be. He would never be able to lift Shiva's bow in this lifetime or any other. He had never accepted humiliation; he had mingled well among the princes at the swayamvara, and decided to adopt a new tactic.

'"Friends!" he proclaimed to the thousands in the Assembly Hall as well as outside. "This contest is a hoax!" There was a chorus of gasps followed by muttering. Janaka in his wisdom remained seated. Had he stood up, the guards would have taken it as a signal that the security of the kingdom was under threat. Janaka, advised by his ministers and sages, wanted to hear the claims of this contestant. "You hear me? *We*, all of you and I, have been cheated. We have been seduced by the glamorous hospitality of Mithila. Our senses have been dulled. What has really happened is that we have been tricked into believing that any one of us could actually lift Shiva's bow. King Janaka does not wish to marry away his daughter

Sita, so he has made us look like fools, while he will gain the status of King of Kings and retain his daughter!"

'A storm of mutterings, gasps and grunts filled the Assembly Hall. Those who were horrified gasped and grunted at these accusations; they were mostly the courtiers of Mithila and its neighbouring allies. But there were mutterings of agreement from some of the demoralized princes and their entourages who were relieved that someone had the courage to say what they were too cowardly to express. The word "cheated" was a great release of frustration and there was a chorus of approval. The wiry prince gained confidence. He had supporters. He realized it was only a matter of language that would turn the tide of popularity in his favour. So he cried, "How do we know, my brothers and friends, those of you who believe what I say and those of you who cannot peel the scales from your eyes, how do you know that at this very moment the gateways to your kingdoms are safe from the rampaging armies of Mithila? Can we guarantee that our mothers, sisters, daughters and the women of our subjects are not being raped and slaughtered in their sleep while we are being held hostage with this hospitality?"

'Janaka stood up with a start—which I could tell was because of a twinge in the right calf muscle caused by an old injury—and this of course signalled a contradictory message. The wiry prince was quick and with clenched fists he raised his arm and cried "WAR!" There were hundreds of fists rising in the Assembly Hall, the rings on their fingers glinting like torches that would spread a forest fire, and the cry was unanimous: "WARRRRRRRRRRRR!" In one nanosecond, the tide of celebration and festivity had turned into hostility that could lead to destruction.

'I was delighted at the effect Ravana's presence had on this assembly. How dull and boring it would have been if everything had gone the way everyone hoped it would. Hope! So sentimental and human. But, amidst all this, I could hear the thoughts stirring within Vishwamitra. "That's all an atom of thought takes to explode—a nanosecond," thought Vishwamitra as he witnessed the scene. "How human reaction can swing from one mode of behaviour to another, and how one dominant person can seize the moment and change the tide of human history for better or for worse. I must do something now."

'Vishwamitra was tall and, even though he stood on the sidelines, he was visible from all corners of the Assembly Hall. He was quick as a flash. In that one split second, when all eyes and voices were focusing on "war" in the direction in which Janaka stood, Vishwamitra too raised his arm, but his palm was open, facing the angry crowds.

'It was customary that when the archbishop of sages such as Vishwamitra made a gesture, everyone took notice and the sheer authority of his presence reduced the shouting to mumbling. There was a hush. Rama was summoned. Vishwamitra signalled all this by his eyes. No words were spoken. Rama was very young, with hardly any hair on his chest. He had no entourage of court singers or masseurs to give him moral or physical support. He had little idea that this contest led to a prize that entailed a lifelong commitment. He looked upon it more as a specific mission his guru had entrusted him with, and knew that he must focus on the task at hand. Everyone was mesmerized by his litheness. But they were convinced that they were going to witness an act of gross misjudgement and decided to hold Vishwamitra responsible for a brave and beautiful warrior ending up dead as a dung beetle.

'Rama bent down and touched the base of the bow with his head. Silence. He lifted it with both hands. Deeper silence. Then, standing the bow on its side, his fingertips slid down the length of the bowstring and up again. The incredible and subtle power of his fingertips made the bow of Shiva crack in two! It was unbelievable. The musicians instantly expressed joy: their instruments began to play of their own accord. The dancers spun. The courtiers forgot their puffy manners and began a rhythmic clapping that crescendoed into an ovation.

'At that moment Sita came spiralling down a jasmine-and-marigold-bedecked sandalwood stairway in short and quick steps accompanied by her ladies-in-waiting.

She had heard the snap of the bow like a thunderbolt and was curious, so she lifted her head and looked over at Rama. "That's him! He's the one who threw the ball that had fallen from my balcony back to me from the street below. The man who stole my heart!" she exclaimed to herself. She was now trembling with relief that he was the bridegroom. This man whose name was on everyone's lips—"Rama!" She willingly inscribed it in her heart, that very name—Rama, whispered with every breath, whether waking or asleep. It shook the very earth beneath her feet. Or was it just thunder rumbling to bring a burst of rain to shower blessings on this marriage?

'I caught up with Ravana later that evening. He sat in his royal apartments on the outskirts of Mithila. I could see the flames from the torchlit streets and the liveried elephants glistening in the distance. Ravana was drinking and for the first time I saw my brother feeling defeated. I was disgusted. How could he bring himself to this lowly human condition? I prodded him.

'"Anna! What an amazing effect you had on that assembly! They are all such complacent brats thinking the world will go on with everyone falling in line! But there you were, letting them know war was close at hand. A timely trick—creating suspicion. It really turned the tide."

'"Yes, and Vishwamitra turned the tide too, didn't he?" replied my brother sarcastically.

'"Don't you think it was all staged? Calling that young chap, Rama?" I had to switch to double deceit as I really thought Rama was yes, inexperienced, but had a spark, a gorgeousness I so desired to possess, or at least to corrupt. He was strong, silent and charming. I dared not show Ravana that this man was worth my attention. Who knows what he would have done. "Hardly any hair on his chest and he is led to the bow. I think Vishwamitra set him up and said a few mantras and those vibrations lifted the bow. Anna, you have met Shiva, you know that bow like your favourite catapult that we used to play with as children to bring vultures down like mere sparrows!"

'Ravana threw his goblet of wine at the servant rakshasa; it struck him on his head and he started to bleed. Ravana roared. He stood and screamed, kicking the table that landed in a great crash that made everything shake. Even my toes grew talons to dig into the floor to steady myself. Then he sat and, his voice going all soft, said,

'"I looked at her. She was the prize, that Sita. Worst of all, did you see the way she looked at him? That fellow with hardly any hair on his chest whom they call a man? Her every breath held tight in her breast so that he would breathe life into her. That was love. How dare he steal her heart? Her heart that would have been mine. I cannot bear it!"

'For the first time I saw how desire was the single thread that held human and rakshasa together. How great its fire was, how the breath of life fanned it, how the rains could never drench it and the desert sun could not scorch it. I saw how like dry wood it was kindled with just one look, and here, for my brother, it was taking an unfathomable direction. He wanted to drink her in and, more importantly, be drunk by her. He was on dangerous territory. He wanted the one thing all of us rakshasas found unspeakable—love. Love in the human heart turns divine. Total surrender! Unspeakable treachery!

'For the first time in all my lives I saw how crushed Ravana was by a woman, named Sita.'

Lakshmana

The minty smell combined with a citrus oil and its tingling sensation made his skin crawl back to life. Then he felt the gentle warmth of a soft, furrowed palm whisking around his face, yet barely touching his fragile skin. Lakshmana lay limp as his legs were crushed under the weight of the chariot's axle. That is all he saw in his mind's eye. Tumbling. Horses, manes, reins. Tumbling in an eternal waterfall. His breath falling after them as he fell in slow motion; like a trapeze artist defying gravity he gave a martial leap in the air before the earth drew him. He did not try to break his fall. The chariot did, as it dismantled when he rode off the track in furious speed, fighting the heart in his throat and the blood and tears blinding his eyes.

That was some years ago. But to him it was a minute ago. After years of a death-sleep, his skin now began to awaken. His eyes did not open. But the palm that stroked the air around his skin brought back an unforgettable memory.

The sound of *Om Namo* hovering around him like a bee single-mindedly approaching a flower also reminded Lakshmana of another time. He could hear the clashing and bashing of clubs and thighs as he recalled that time. It came back vividly with the sound of splitting skulls and screeching monkeys while vultures and other birds of prey picked the long braids of intestines oozing like sticky red thread out of the wounded. He could see all this now with his eyes closed. But he had once seen it with his eyes open. He was on a battlefield. It was difficult to see and he was losing blood and breath. In that fetid air he came under an enormous shadow that blocked the sun. It wasn't a cloud. All the monkeys were gnashing their teeth in terror, until they were engulfed by the shadow of a tail whisking in the air. A few minutes after the shadow passed over the battlefield, there was a giant thud followed by what felt like earthquake. Once more, the hooting and hollering from the armies of the bears and the monkeys started. Lakshmana was paralysed and could only hear: HAN-U-MAN, HAN-U-MAN, HAN-U-MAN. He could feel the heavy footsteps and the thumping tail. Hanuman had brought the mountain with the sanjeevini herb. The minty smell mixed with the citrus oil on the gently furrowed palm of the hand wafted into his nostrils and he felt the occasional brush of fur. Was this from a memory or was it in the present?

Lakshmana opened his battered eyes. It wasn't the past, it wasn't a dream. 'It was, it is, Hanuman,' he heard in his head. He could only let out a grunt that was stifled by the pain radiating from his bruised and blistered skin. Hanuman looked back at him the way gorillas gaze into the near distance—understanding human reactions, but not necessarily giving the expected responses. His eyes were red and his breathing was almost still as he gently placed his hairy ear close to Lakshmana's chest. Hanuman could hear the broken ribs, sounding like pebbles grating when they are dragged from the shore into the sea. Lakshmana's moans indicated a new language. Hanuman listened to the story bubbling and bursting through Lakshmana, who had words flowing within him that could only come out as crushed sounds.

'I can see now how I arrived here. No, not the way my body is crushed. That was only an accident. But what led to it. It is also the way we first met you, Hanuman.

'In Panchavati, in that last stage of our exile. I was busy sharpening my arrows up on the tree watchtower when I heard a commotion down below. I was wondering how I could have let this happen. I had actually fallen off to sleep and was dreaming I was sharpening my arrows! I prayed to Nidra, the goddess of sleep, and begged her not to visit me so often. I was on a mission; at any time of day we could be attacked so I needed to be fresh and alert. Just at that moment I heard Rama say: "But, dear lady, my brother Lakshmana has been alone all these years. Why not ask him?" And so, Soorpanakka, in a bewitching form with plaited hair down to her waist, threaded with jasmines and gems, swayed seductively towards me. I knew something was afoot, so grabbing my sword I leapt down. She looked at me and said, "Look I can offer you anything: armies, navies, elephants, gold beyond your dreams and desire. It's not really you I have come after. But at least if I am married to you, I will make it a family affair!" She winked. "That's enough. I know you are a rakshasa and I command you to leave this place at once," I said, "or else."

"'Or else what?" was her taunting reply, and she came closer. Her body swayed, she was nearly pressed against me. I remember the touch. I could smell the perfume of the jasmines, and the next instant when she opened her mouth it was the stench of stale fish. She taunted me with the fact that I knew she was a rakshasa but was being chivalrous to her in her acquired shape as a woman. When I looked at Rama, he was smiling mischievously at Sita and they seemed unaware of what Soorpanakka was saying to me. She had cast her spell. Desire was welling up in her eyes; I was just another conquest. She knew I knew so she shifted strategy.

"'Even if you did not notice me, I was there at the swayamvara. I longed for you. You, who are so strong and silent, and yet always put yourself down for your brother. That chit of a girl you were forced to marry . . .'"

"'That's enough! Urmilla is my wife. Be grateful to her that I've put up with you for so long—I could never strike a woman, thanks to her!' I was being drawn into a web of useless words. She had clamped me with an unseen power that felt like a crocodile's grip.

"'Well, if you love your brother and that wife of his so much then steel yourself and listen to some truths. Kaikeyi is not to blame for this exile. It is your father who seems to have forgotten his word of honour.'

'I was enraged that she brought my father into this taunt. She could measure my temper when I snapped "How dare you!"

"'Oh! Your ridiculous threats. Dare? Dare? Has your wife ever dared anything? Well, I dare your honour to hear a few unsavoury facts. Kaikeyi was beautiful and young. Your father, after having married Kausalya, went on one of his campaigns to prove how powerful he still was even if he could not have a child. Of course, when he saw Kaikeyi, the daughter of King Keykeya, Dasaratha was constantly aroused by her bewitching beauty. Keykeya's neighbouring kingdom was becoming a threat to Kaikeyi's father, so Dasaratha decided to wage war to show his loyalty in the hope of winning Kaikeyi for himself. Kaikeyi, so desperately in love, in spite of herself, drove your father's chariot into battle against Keykeya's enemy. No one wishes to reveal the story of the time when one of the wheels of Dasaratha's chariot got stuck in the mud. Kaikeyi, his charioteer, held the chariot with her back and by propping it up against a rock. Your father, Dasaratha, then in face-to-face combat, slit his enemy's throat. When the battle ended and he was victorious, Dasaratha swept Kaikeyi off her feet and held her face with his bloodied hands, drew her into his arms and kissed her until she agreed to marry him. King Keykeya got your father to sign and seal a scroll where he agreed to make Kaikeyi's child the heir to the throne."

'It was all so surreal. Rama and Sita, though within earshot, couldn't hear any of this, and there was I, being fed a story that turned the soil of all the relationships by which I felt rooted. Yet, there was something compelling about Soorpanakka and what she told me. I wondered what was the moral ground on which Rama and all of us stood? It was subject to the story that we had been told by our father. And here we were, giving our youth, our lives, to honour his word. And from what I was being told, the word was false. So what was different between us and the rakshasas? They believed in their untruths; there was a kind of honesty about it. And here we had been fed myths about righteousness; I felt so much for Bharata. How I had doubted him. And there was my Urmilla caught up in this churning ocean of life because of my belief in honour. Sita too. But at least Sita's choice to accompany him was accepted by Rama. I had rebuked Urmilla for even suggesting that she wanted to be beside me in exile, telling her she would be a liability in the forest. I felt nauseous. I don't know what possessed me. I felt the blood rising and throbbing in my temples. All I heard Soorpanakka say was: "Or else?"

'That was like the sound of the conch for commencing battle. I flew into such a rage that I raised the sword and chopped off her nose and ears. The hideous attack made her flee. She had not imagined I would do it. Neither had I. I had been provoked. I wonder whether it was to avenge my feeling of betrayal. I felt betrayed by my father who had made me doubt my brother Bharata and everything I had been certain about till that moment. Sensing the danger of the effect it could have on Rama, on Sita, as we had sacrificed our youth to honour our father's word, I panicked and lashed out. It was only then that Rama and Sita looked. They looked with horror. What they saw was so different from how I saw it because they did not hear what I did. Did I have the additional responsibility of keeping quiet about it? And now, the final sting—Rama's remark about me being lonely all these years without Urmilla in the forest! Sita was shocked and sick at the sight of the fleeing Soorpanakka. Rama knelt, holding Sita's head as she crouched on the ground.

'That was when I saw the goddess of sleep, Nidra, approaching. My lids were heavy, and she looked so comforting with her wide lap. I commanded her to stop in her tracks. I had to be more alert from now on. I knew Soorpanakka's encounter with me would be followed by more skirmishes in the Panchavati forest. Nidra was, after all, fulfilling her role. What would we be if we did not sleep? I then begged her to put Urmilla to sleep until my return. But Nidra would charge a fee for granting my wish. So she made me accept she would return to me when she thought it fit. I bargained. She could not visit me while we were in the final stage of exile. She protested that it would be so unnatural. All the goddesses of health would blame her. Finally, she gave in to my request of visiting me after Rama had returned to Ayodhya and been crowned king.

'When you have a stomach ache you try to remember what you have eaten; every problem has an origin. I kept telling myself to be alert and not let Soorpanakka slip past me again.

'Then came the golden deer and Sita was transfixed and insistent on Rama going after it. I have thought many times of that crocodile-like grip of Soorpanakka when she had taunted me. Was it the same kind of spell under which Sita had fallen? But when she heard the cry that she believed was Rama's, she became her former self. For one moment I saw her so vulnerable and completely subsumed by her concern for Rama. She had forgotten the dangers of the forest and cared nothing for herself. She begged me to go, and, just as I came towards her, visibly moved by her love for my brother, she launched an attack: "My beloved is dying and all you can do is stand here with your arms folded in resignation while you sweet-talk me about the great exploits of your brother Rama? Yes, he may have killed Tataka and lifted Shiva's bow, but now his life is in danger and you are delaying rescuing him? What's the matter with you? Is this the time you have been waiting for to show your real intention towards me?" Her words struck me worse than poisoned darts. I had never seen her eyes flash fire and her mouth utter such filth. Did she say that to provoke me? I drew the lakshman rekha around her to protect her and ran in the direction Rama had taken in pursuit of that fateful golden deer.

'After all that happened and we returned to Ayodhya, it was a few months into the reign of Rama. We were all at court. Sugriva had come to visit; Vibhishana was also there. I was gazing on the scene when the court poets were singing of Rama's glory. Suddenly I felt my eyelids grow very heavy. I saw her—Nidra. She smiled. I nodded. I had forgotten what she looked like or, indeed, who she was. It had been nearly two and a half years since we had made that bargain. She did as promised. But, of course, in her unique way, she came unannounced. To visit me, in style, at court. I felt as if I had lost all control over my body and its senses. It was a dizzy and warm feeling. Almost like being happily inebriated. I was listening to the songs of praise recounting the bravery of the human race and the greatness of man and civilization. I started to smile. My muscles were relaxing. Years of constant vigil and staying awake began to fly away and with it, the tension. I laughed and put my hand to my mouth. The laughter started taking over. I couldn't suppress it any longer behind my cupped hand. I laughed out loud. It was an unbelievable force that took over and I was deliriously happy. There were murmurs and sounds of shuffling. At first the singers, who were also great Wits, felt complimented. They interpreted my laughter as attentive listening to their puns, conundrums and nuances. But I wasn't laughing on cue. So they started to look at each other, stumbling over their lines and faltering, and shied away into finishing the recitation as soon as was possible. I tried to explain, but no words would come out, only rippling laughter.

'I saw Rama at first humouring me, but then running out of breath and possibly losing his patience. I could see the laughter was getting to him, because he thought I was laughing at him. He grew reflective. Sugriva, who was offering Rama an ambassadorial tribute, too felt self-conscious and began to reflect on that time when he had regained his kingdom. He wondered if I was laughing at him for being drunk and unprepared with his army, and how we had to wait out the monsoon before he came to our rescue to find Sita. In his embarrassment he pulled at his ear and the earring fell out. It went clattering down on the stone steps, spinning like a top towards Rama's throne. Sugriva clambered down after it; when he picked it up, his regal but monkeyish awkwardness made me laugh even more.

'Vibhishana, on hearing my laughter, began to think whether he might go down in the chronicles of history as a usurper of Ravana's kingdom. He kept looking down as if he was considering for the first time how the people of Ayodhya, perhaps even the generations to come, might feel about him becoming the king of Lanka. Was he a good rakshasa or was that really a question to be considered? But my laughter would not show any respect for his doubts and wavering, or indeed his bravery. I could not stop laughing.

'Kausalya Amma was present but began to worry about why she was still alive when her husband was dead.

'Bharata wanted to calm me down as now it was distracting everyone in the Assembly Hall. He was worried I was laughing at him for not having ruled the kingdom well or indeed because he had run the country like a monastery while Rama, Sita and I were away. I could see what he was thinking by watching his expressions, and that made me laugh even louder because he should have known better about how much he was admired; but, at that moment, it was so funny that he could not see it and kept putting himself down.

'Sita at first wondered what had brought this about. Then she wondered if the war was making me feel ill and whether she was worth all the lives lost in the battle. But then she looked straight at me and said, "Lakshmana, it has been fourteen long years. You have not slept as you kept constant vigil over Rama and me. Had it not been for you, *we* would not have been blessed with sleep. Your supreme sacrifice was that you did not see or speak with Urmila as she had cast herself into a deep sleep until your return. Now hurry, make up for lost time and be by her side."

'I could now see Nidra dancing around. I was reeling with laughter and could not help thinking how the goddess of sleep had nothing to do with inertia; sleep was a source of energy. But with her approach everybody becomes cautious, even reflective. I realized that Nidra is the keeper of our secrets, which, in waking, we are not even aware of. When she descends, she churns the ocean of memories that lies deep within, and we start to see ourselves in a way that we have forgotten to when awake. I also remember saluting her because much as I had prayed to her to stay away and thought I had won final control when she did not return, her timing had finally exposed me in public! I was the prince who never slept, who had conquered sleep. That was really something to laugh about—about who was really in control. Sita was the only one who could see that I was dancing with Nidra. She saw my laughter was not intended as a show of superiority and to make others feel uncomfortable. It was about losing control and surrendering.

'It was then that I left the court and slept soundly. How many days passed, I have no count of; there is no chronology in sleep. People, places, events tumble in from top-down and sideways. I had so much dream-time to catch up on. I had not met Rama properly since. I remember waking up and rushing out to meet the hunters. When I returned, it was already too late.

'I heard Rama's decision. I could not convince him against it. I slept at the most crucial moment of Sita's life. And when I brought her to the forest and was told to

abandon her so Rama could prove to his people that . . .
I don't know what he wanted to prove; I could not punish
her like that. It amounted to deceit. Even if he thought
people would come around and want their queen back,
how could Rama ignore Sita's feelings? Or had he taken
her for granted? Like most men who expect their wives
to fit into a mould! He always told me Sita was different.
She was not a woman who expected to be tossed around
in the maelstrom of misfortune. He had always insisted
she would be the one to light the dawn of a new age for
women. Then to hear this decision of his . . .

'Valmiki was the safest option. I left her there. Even
though I could not look back, I could imagine her standing
there, one hand clasping the other. Stunned into stone the
way Ahalya was. I had always feared the fire in her eyes,
like the time she commanded me to light the fire when
Rama rebuked her in Lanka. It was worse to imagine she
had turned to stone. I knew I could not drive back to the
kingdom and face Rama and his dual lives of state and
self, stretched like wet leather in the sun. I had nowhere
else to go but to die.

'The lightness of the air, of so much sleep after so
much wakefulness, made me leap into nothingness. My
body flung itself like a tongue in the laughing mouth of
the ravine. I found nothing in myself to redeem after what
had happened to Sita, and I am left with nothing.'

Hanuman heard all this through the wheezing and moaning and troubled breathing of Lakshmana.

Some leaves parted, as a deer munched its way through. Hanuman and the deer gazed at each other as their nostrils quivered to seek the essential scent of the other, distinguishing prey from predator.

Hanuman

Hanuman wept. In his stillness he had heard every creak, sigh, groan, trickle, whisper, and seen a flood of images forcing their way through Lakshmana's story. So great were Hanuman's powers of understanding breath. He continued anointing Lakshmana's broken skin with the herb ointment and sealed it with the porous pith of a plantain tree. It became a hammock that generated and cradled new skin; it also looked like a shroud. Hanuman wept his animal-human tears watching Lakshmana's broken body resisting any kind of treatment. But more than that, he howled from within on hearing the way Lakshmana's bones were crushed under the weight of his unnecessary guilt.

The air was humid. Lakshmana was thirsty. He was overwhelmed by the sheer exhaustion of being kept alive over the years by wandering ascetics before Hanuman discovered him. Hanuman's tears ran down his furry cheek and formed a steady drip and seeped between the cracks of Lakshmana's battered lips. The salty sweetness of the moisture must have burned; Lakshmana's broken skin flinched. Hanuman was relieved his body was still responding. He knew all too well the struggle between the tenacious urge to live and the desire to die. The greatest difficulty was that fiery particle, the mind. It would not let go of memory, association, status and the great pyramid of entombing itself with the loose-footed grasp of sensory things.

During all that time in which they had known each other, Hanuman had been the real insider to Sita's story, and only he had known Lakshmana's place within it. Hanuman could only speak with his eyes. Lakshmana could sense every word. Hanuman could not help feeling pained, and slighted, that Lakshmana did not contact him with the mantra they shared for danger signals ever since the sanjeevini herb incident—*especially about the mission to banish Sita*. Hanuman would have reasoned with Rama against his fears. Hanuman knew Rama's fears and loved him in spite of them. He knew Rama to be a wise and compassionate leader. Rama, in his bouts of gloom after being separated from Sita, hovered around thinking the right thought, whether it was solely for the individual, or the collective good, and acting swiftly upon it. Hanuman also sensed Rama's discomfort with being constantly judged in the public eye, in the present and the future. Rama was often tormented by the possibility that whatever he did would set an example that others would follow, and in varied contexts it could stigmatize him.

Hanuman also knew Lakshmana would never advise Rama against his darker moments, because that would seem like undermining an older brother's authority. 'Even when it was about shedding more light on a subject! Human courtesies often went too far in killing one's instinct, or do they call it "spontaneity"?' thought Hanuman. But more than that, Hanuman could not bear to see Lakshmana's life ebbing away because he mistakenly burdened himself with the guilt of being the cause of Sita's abduction.

Hanuman could see deeper under the layers of stories that would be chronicled and told for ages to come, that the truth lay in Lakshmana's reticence. Hanuman was a pioneer in espionage in Sugriva's kingdom, and he could detect that in Lakshmana's case, it wasn't the miscalculation of being in the wrong place at the wrong time; it was about a feeling of rejection and loss ever since that moment that paved the way for the abduction.

Lakshmana's breathing was all Hanuman needed to map the dark forest of the invalid's being. In fact, he was reconstructing the fibre of his skin cell by cell. It was the word 'abduction' that seemed to rankle Lakshmana the most. Hanuman wondered if facing the truth was what was holding him back. 'Abduction' was a word amongst humans that threw them into a black hole of confusion, fear, despair and hatred. There was a collective view of defining and thinking about abduction. Abduction carried the weight of someone being taken against their will, and yet it was also about surrendering against their will.

All those years ago, that fatal afternoon, the golden deer had flitted into the thick of the forest with Rama determined to capture it for Sita. He was undecided at first, but Sita turned on him and said: 'That deer could be our souvenir of all this time that we've spent in the forest. I've never asked anything of you these last thirteen years, and even this one thing seems so difficult, is it? . . . Oh! What's the use! That enchanting deer has fled!' The last thing Rama uttered was: 'Lakshmana, make sure Sita comes to no harm! I will return.'

After a while, following the tunnel of shrieks and wails of birds and monkeys, the afternoon was wrenched apart by terrifying cries in what sounded like Rama's voice. Lakshmana saw how distraught Sita became when she heard Rama's voice; she was consumed by her concern for

Rama. She looked so vulnerable, without a sense of her self. In that shining moment he saw the totality of Rama and Sita's love, which transcended boundaries of body and space. It was an epiphany that washed through him like a wave buoying him from his finite body to an immersion in infinity. Something in Lakshmana's expression indicated his longing to belong to that infinity. He sighed—an expression of wonder at having witnessed something so sublime. Sita turned as she heard him sigh and was distracted by his look of pain and longing. She coded another signal. Longing for the infinite, translated through his finite body, was read by Sita as temporal desire. The infinity that Lakshmana had perceived in Sita was being manifested through a woman's body experiencing loss, fear, love and anger. As Sita's eyes flashed with anger, Lakshmana saw her infinity merging and constricting itself into the finite. 'Is this the time you have found to look at me?' was her first utterance. He was speechless. What had at first enraptured him now eroded into something so base. Yet, both were expressions of the same body. He now felt *abducted* by a power greater than himself and it seemed he was surrendering himself to it against his will. His sense of loss brought his characteristic impatience to the surface, and in an act of love and despair he drew the lakshman rekha, a laser circle to protect Sita as long as she stayed within its circumference.

When he ran towards Rama, his thoughts were flying in all directions, churning the years of selfhood that he had created. So, when he returned with Rama to encounter the reality of Sita's abduction, he was totally consumed by a wave of guilt. It was not because of what had happened, but by the tangible sense of having been abducted by something beyond him and having become powerless. Sita had seen through it, and now Hanuman could sense through his pulse how deeply that anguish had filtered into Lakshmana's being; Hanuman could hear it in his very breathing. Lakshmana always felt second best and more so when Hanuman came into the frame of the relationship between the brothers, and that much more did he feel abducted by guilt for leaving Sita alone. Rama never once rebuked Lakshmana, and that weighed heavily too. Hanuman alone knew the extent of Rama's love for Lakshmana.

The deer that was peering at Hanuman gained confidence and came closer. Hanuman looked into its past lives and discerned that in none of them was it a rakshasa, or capable of shape-shifting. 'But what of Sita, where could she be now?' he thought.

Hanuman had learnt over the years that if one had to go in search of something, even a spiritual quest, it had to be done by following some clues, however random they seemed. It was only after the mission had begun that he could find the reason or purpose behind the quest. For him, the first thing was to know the quality of the person or the quest that he was seeking. When he went to seek Sita in Lanka it was clearly because of his love of Rama that he set out on that mission. When he met Sita, he was ready to turn Lanka upside down for the suffering that Ravana had caused her. Hanuman had seen Sita the way no one else had, or could. In captivity too she was brave, never giving in to Ravana's manipulative logic, shape-shifting and delusions. She had shared her anguish about the state of corruption that was embedded in everyone who visited her. 'If this way of being takes over, what will become of the future?' she had sighed when they both sat under that tree in Asokavan.

He thought of the three symbols associated with Sita. The first was the iron bow granted by Shiva. It was impossibly large, unwieldy and sure to fail any contestant—human, animal or divine. But Sita having discovered it in the vegetable garden was able to pluck it out like a weed from the earth. He marvelled at how she knew the real trick—it wasn't about physical strength. It was about sheer mental and spiritual grit. Determination. That was the magic formula in Shiva's bow. Not for acclaim or physical prowess but for the accomplishment of the task at hand. Hanuman, who was an avatar of Shiva born to Anjani and Kesari, knew this.

The second symbol was the ring that Sita had given Rama when they had married. The gem was a deep forest-green emerald and the gold filigree around the band held an inscription which read:

My earth, my moon, my sun. Rama, my full circle.

After the war, even after that fateful agnipariksha fire trial, Rama continued to wear the ring. Hanuman would often catch him musing at sunset. He would press it close to his lip as if Sita's ring held his life in its eternal circle.

'Why then would Rama make this preposterous decision? Dirt can cover gold, but it will not affect its purity. On the other hand, doubt, like a black speck within a diamond cannot be removed . . .' Hanuman twisted and turned many arguments till his head started to spin.

The third symbol was the scrap of Sita's sari that he had preserved as a relic. He had never had the time to ask her whether she had torn it as a clue for Rama to come in search of her when she was being carried away; or whether Ravana in his scramble tore it and it fell; or indeed when the aerial chariot was rising in the air and Jatayu challenged Ravana mid-air, the sari got ripped by the branch of a tree and slid down with the heavy rains that followed? Did it matter that it would never be known?

Hanuman placed Lakshmana's crushed body in a hammock created of pith, soft grass and feathers, leaves and abandoned bird-nests. He ensured that the hammock was suspended between the sturdy branches of two low-lying boughs and anointed him with a powerful mantra so no beast or human would attack him. Hanuman was on a mission. He decided to seek Valmiki. He wanted to know the truth—why does human understanding in such ideal relationships get corrupted, and how does it happen?

The important thing was to tell Sita's story. When he sat with her in Asokavan in Lanka, Hanuman had offered to end her trials by taking her back to Rama. But she was insistent that he return to Rama alone, with her fervent conviction. 'It's not about me,' she had said. 'Rama and Ravana have to face each other. Rama is single-minded and wedded to the truth. Ravana has myriads of distractions, and he continues to delude himself that power is the real source of knowledge. He believes that corrupting power to suit his own ends will make him immortal. My returning with you would be "safe". But what would Rama have signalled to the rest of the world? I sometimes wish we were down to earth in our aspirations. But no, it's not enough. Things have to be stirred at the very root. To me, this is about my abduction, yes; but it is also about being avenged. Why should anyone, human or animal, be used as a pawn? Why am I a pawn in this game of creating alliances and oppositions between forces? Why is the focus a woman's vulnerability? Why not her strength as a bargaining power for peace—even if by means of war?

'I'm not weak, Hanuman, I know what I have endured. The rakshasis hate me, perhaps the whole world despises me. I can rise above what is to come, but I'm no martyr. The real test is to come after all this, in spite of all this. It is up to you, Rama, me, all of us to rebuild a world of trust with the seeds of our belief. A world without trust will never have the strength to seek the truth. Without the quest for truth there is no love—and dear, dear Hanuman, without love this life is meaningless. That is the cycle of the birth and death of hopelessness that I want my freedom from. Ra-ma!' She sighed. The name, the being, the man, her love—it was her life-breath.

When the war got over, Hanuman ran swiftly to Asokavan to meet Sita. He needed to see her in person and tell her that Rama was alive and Ravana was dead. He knew about the various tricks Ravana had played on her. He might even have got one of the rakshasi attendants to misinform Sita of the turn of events after he was killed. As he reached Asokavan where she was still being held hostage, he found her sitting alone with the look of someone who had endured too much and was close to tipping over the edge of sanity. She was gazing mindlessly at a crow that was plucking a red strand of intestine; its beak was stained with blood.

The first words Hanuman uttered had to be carefully chosen. She saw him and stood up. Her legs were giving way. At the verge of herself, she asked, 'Is it all over? And . . . him?' Hanuman quickly said, 'Rama . . .' and she began twisting and wringing the palla of the sari she had been wearing since the time she had been captured. She was very agitated and it seemed to Hanuman she was making a rope to hang herself with, thinking that it was Rama who had been slain. In the distance when the conch shells sounded, she looked again at Hanuman. Her eyes once again sparked with life when he finally spilled the good news. She cried with relief. Triumph, victory, nothing mattered. To know that Rama was alive poured the very essence of life back into her. Her voice, her limbs, everything was restored. 'I'll keep this sari for as long as I live; wherever I am. Its every wrinkle is inscribed with all my longing for Rama to return. Return to the Light!' Hanuman wept too, inaudibly uttering *Jai Sita Ram*.

When they were back in Ayodhya, many months later, Rama and Sita were settling into a pattern of domestic life in a city after years of roaming in the forest. Hanuman was visiting and stayed for a while. He would help Sita clear her vegetable garden and they both talked of many things, ordinary and extraordinary. It was often for an hour after lunch. One day, as Hanuman approached, he saw another woman sitting beside Sita and reading her palm. She appeared to be a mendicant with numerous little bundles tied to a forked stick. Gifted with an inner vision for reading the invisible aura of beings, Hanuman could tell this was Soorpanakka in a shape-shifted form.

He tuned into their conversation. 'It won't be long now. You'll be pregnant,' said Soorpanakka, 'and all the trials you suffered in captivity will be washed away.' Sita gasped at the foresight of the stranger but was captivated by her soothsaying. The mendicant continued, 'So, tell me, they say he held you for one whole year in captivity? Surely, you could have found a way to escape? I suppose he kept watch on you night and day. Or perhaps he watched over you himself! So, what do you now remember of Ravana?'

'Nothing, really,' replied Sita as she was thinning some sandalwood to make a paste to anoint Rama on his return home.

'Really? Was there really nothing that tormented you? Whatever his faults, he must have been very remarkable!' Soorpanakka pursued Sita.

'I never looked at him,' said Sita plainly.

'But you must have heard his voice? Heard his footsteps as he walked towards your cell, shifting his weight from one foot to the other, or even recognized his perfume?' And so, on and on Soorpanakka in the garb of a stranger persuaded Sita to confide in her. 'Many palaces lingered with his perfume long after he had left.'

'That may have been so. But I was subsumed by what had happened to me in one blinding flash that afternoon in the forest. All I had was the memory of Rama, waving to me, then rushing into the depths of the forest. What madness I sent him towards—a golden deer! What was I thinking? That was the last image I had of Rama, and it was all I clung to. Rama, night and day, day and night.'

'Surely, you took in what was around you? There was a possibility during the twilight hours?' asked Soorpanakka mischievously.

'As I never looked at anything, I cannot tell you.' Sita paused. She remembered looking beyond. 'But just once, I remember seeing his toenail,' she said, as if not wanting to leave her guest empty-handed in her search.

Hanuman, watching through the trees, winced. As he moved forward, he felt something tumbling inside him. The feeling of arriving too late.

'Describe it to me,' whispered Soorpanakka. Sita began: 'It was oval and shone like mother-of-pearl. It was like a mirror . . . he must have wanted to look at himself at all times.' The woman started to draw. 'I'll complete this and return it to you tomorrow,' said the mendicant Soorpanakka as she deftly rolled all her bundles into one big mop and, casting it on her shoulder, began to sway out of Sita's vegetable garden.

Hanuman kept watch. The next day when the stranger visited Sita, she unravelled a portrait of Ravana on cloth. Sita was taking down her exile sari that had been drying, and Soorpanakka quickly rolled the painting with a smaller section of the sari.

When Hanuman met her the next day, Sita told him what happened. They both peered at the open scroll. It had a line drawing of Ravana standing, dressed in all his splendour. The tone was compassionate, as was the subject, in spite of his magnificent attire; he looked down at his polished toenail, almost as if to catch Sita's eye in it. Hanuman could see Sita's predicament. 'I don't know what to do. She saw me and predicted that I would be pregnant. How can I turn away a well-wisher, even if she was only a passerby, just like that, Hanuman? In giving me the good news she also wanted to make me a present, but I did not know what kind of present. I just gave her one word . . . a toenail.'

'And we are confronted with our inner warrior to wrestle with our conscience,' said Hanuman almost inaudibly. Then, in his inimitable way of being decisive but hesitating out of courtesy, asked: 'Can you not destroy it?'

'What if more harm comes from it? Surely, it's not good to do that with someone's creation? And that too of a woman's who has spells and charms!'

It seemed to Hanuman that Sita had been thinking of how to hide the scroll from Rama for a good part of the day. She kept it under her bed, hidden in her wooden dowry chest. That night she dreamt the painting had come to life. Ravana emerged from the scroll and stretched and yawned as if he had been in a temporary sleep and had awoken refreshed. As he stretched, he caught hold of Sita's sari palla and started unravelling it; she was losing control. He smiled lasciviously and drew her so close she could smell his perfume, and his breath, and she began to scream. Sita awoke with a start and did not know what to say as Rama held her very close, even tightly. Rama wondered what the matter was.

The very next day, Sita decided she must get rid of the scroll. She had made sure that the maids and cleaners left early that afternoon. It took her considerable effort to drag the dowry chest by one of its side handles; she brought it out, keeping it close to the bed. Her hands were trembling as she steadied the key into the embedded lock. She heard it click and the well-oiled lid of the chest swung open. She bent down to get the scroll that was hidden among some of the things she had collected during exile. She didn't hear the door open, the softness of Rama's feet on the floor as he returned unexpectedly. He was delighted that no one was around. To spend a few moments with Sita, alone, during the day was a rare privilege. He wanted to surprise her and stood still gazing at her. She stood transfixed by the skill of the artist staring back at her from the open scroll as she held it in her outstretched right hand. Rama wanted to surprise her. His arm slipped deftly round her waist and as he drew her close she felt his soft breath on the nape of her neck, until he saw what she had been looking at. She froze and he froze. He moved aside and she turned to face him—her arm still frozen holding the portrait of Ravana. 'You don't understand . . .' she began and stepped towards him, 'it's not what you think . . .' when the scrap of the exile sari slipped from her other hand that she had extended in an attempt to touch him. Rama recoiled; he had never been wounded in this way before. He knew how precious that chest was to her, where she had stored all the things that deeply mattered to her during exile. Seeing the chest unlocked and Ravana's portrait in her hand must have opened a door into the dark for him. Perhaps he did understand what she felt but couldn't understand the situation they were in, tormented by Ravana even after his death. Yet again, there was a bridge between them that could not be crossed. She took one more step towards him and he stood, willing to listen. She could not mistake the love he held for her in his eyes and the open wound in his tears. Outside, the herald sounded the hour and in the hall of the apartment, a minister was announced for his appointment with Rama. One more interruption. All he said was, 'After all that time, Sita, this?' before he turned and left. There was a bridge between them, but now silence was growing thick and fast like the darkness that shrouds any glimmer of the possibility of moving forward.

Hanuman could see it all so clearly when he went to meet Sita the next day. Her eyes had lost their lustre. Rama and Sita never indulged in domestic quarrels that could become the hub of gossip and intrigue along the palace corridors. But he sensed the storms brewing in their interior landscape. Rama was meticulous in his attention to detail at the court, while Sita carried out her duties with an inward gaze. It all looked frighteningly normal.

Hanuman decided he would do something totally by instinct to solve the problem. Once again, he used his special power granted by his father, Vayu, the god of air. He sighed at first, then took a deep breath. He shrank to the size of an ordinary rhesus monkey. The monkey scampered on all fours and began to spoil the ripe plantains hanging from the tree. The gardeners and cleaners tried to chase the menace away, but the monkey leapt on to the veranda of the palace apartment. Scurrying into the royal bedroom, it hid under the bed of Rama and Sita and dragged out the scroll that was lying near the chest. Now there was a longer train of cleaners, maids and stewards who were following the monkey and were determined to catch it. The monkey gnashed its teeth and screeched at everyone who in turn was paralysed into a stunned silence. Then it proceeded to eat the scroll, bit by bit, and then in chunks as it was chased around in the room. With one enormous belch it swung its tail, reached an open window and leapt out of it. With screams and shouts and the train of attendants following in a long shuffle, the monkey reached the plantain grove. It sat and started growing purple. Everyone stood around in a circle seeing it groan. It vomited at the base of the tree. One of the gardeners approached with a flaming stick of wood. The monkey swivelled this way and that and lunged up on to the tree, which had now caught fire, and with a final screech through the smoke, disappeared. No one could tell what had happened to the monkey.

The story of the vanishing monkey was the talk of the domestic staff the whole of the next week. Then the great news broke into the open—Sita, their beloved queen, was pregnant.

Hanuman smiled to himself as he remembered the incident and jogged into a thicker part of the jungle. He came to a custard apple tree and could not resist. He stopped and picked the soft fruit. He placed one in his mouth—it was so creamy and sweet. Whatever the scale of his mission, he couldn't stop himself from playing his game of spitting out the pips. These formed tell-tale arcs that mapped his way from Lakshmana, and through the overgrown trail that led to Valmiki's hermitage.

Ashwamedha

Drums were pounding and conch shells and cymbals were resonating through the streets of Ayodhya. It was an hour before midday. The perambulation around the temple had been completed and the procession had reached the palace lotus pond. The procession had followed a golden idol of Vishnu bedecked with emeralds, rubies, pearls and sapphires seated on a palanquin carried by forty strong brahmins. The bamboo poles of the palanquin, each fifteen feet long and five inches in diameter, rested on their bare shoulders. They deemed it as a mark of the god pressing his feet into their bodies. They heaved with entranced devotion, singing the thousand and one aspects of Vishnu, who to them was the sustainer of life. Ten men each carried the left and right front poles of the palanquin with the space for a man to run between the columns, dowsing them with water in the midday heat. The same arrangement was followed for the two columns of men carrying the rear poles.

A vibrantly embroidered umbrella was fixed above Vishnu's head to protect him from the sun. The procession was a labour of intense love. Vishnu was parading the streets. Women having their periods and elderly men and women stood at their doorways—which were wreathed with branches of neem leaves to mark a sign of illness in the house—as Vishnu and his brahmin warriors passed by, chanting the hymns. All those who could not go to the temple where he resided were now brushed with the god's grace. 'You see, Vishnu loves us. If we cannot go to him, he comes to us!' said a salt seller, her eyes beaming as though by the arrival of a long-awaited parent. The deity on the palanquin rocked on the shoulders of the men who paused by her for one moment. Everyone's heart was brimming over with Vishnu's visit.

Kings from neighbouring kingdoms were on a state visit and Rama was in consultation with his ministers. The fragrance of frankincense mixed with dust and the confetti of marigold petals wafted in through the open arches of the Assembly Hall from the procession on the streets. They couldn't help hearing the exhilarated invocation to Vishnu:

You are the breath of being
You are sound in space
You are wetness of water
You are fragrance of flowers
The butter in milk, churned from the ocean of
consciousness
O let there be Love Eternal
The way You are

Sixty or more years ago, Valmiki had seen a white luminous dot in the middle of a moonless night. The pounding on the earth as he put his ear to the forest floor sang of freedom. Sixty or more years hence, Valmiki could hear it again. A low thunder that would ascend into a torrential happening. This was the Ashwamedha. The name of the ritual that every king would dare to perform if he were invited to, but dare not for the fear of failing. Like his father Dasaratha before him, Rama, counselled by his ablest ministers, agreed to release the luminous white horse from the kingdom's stables. It would gallop without a rider, or a bridle, across the borders of kingdoms. The rulers of these kingdoms had made their alliances and were in the Assembly Hall listening to the invocations to Vishnu, in the hope of hearing that the Ashwamedha horse returned to Ayodhya's stables without being contested. It was a foregone conclusion that Rama, like Dasaratha, would be crowned King of Kings.

Even if there were rebellious kings, no one had dared bridle the Ashwamedha, or ride it, as that would signal a challenge to Rama's rule. Preparations had been taking place for months. The penultimate stage had arrived. The horse rode on for three days and three nights, with Ayodhya's messengers taking outposts at various locations to desist the horse from stalling for too long. They hid behind rocks and hills, within fields and valleys, past the bends along riverbanks, under the arches of gateways in and out of kingdoms, inside monasteries, sanctuaries, granary houses, villages. Messages were flown by courier pigeons and communicated through a code of clay whistles to chart the Ashwamedha's journey and relayed to Ayodhya. Ministers would be given the information after the progress had been confirmed, to collate how many kingdoms had submitted to the alliance with Rama. There was a loud cheer as results declared that in none of the kingdoms represented in the Assembly Hall had the horse been stopped by any rebellious group. Each king beamed with pride as he was honoured for keeping his word and confirming the alliance to Rama's court. The other kings nodded assent. They knew who their allies were in case sub-alliances had to be formed.

The countdown had been going on for months as the horse charted new territories. It was a night with the moon waxing into its third quarter. As the horse galloped onward, its mane flying, it seemed to light up the dark night. In the forest by Ayodhya, parrots, kingfishers, peacocks had all settled for the night. The owls kept watch, and even the daytime birds stirred in their nests as they sensed a change. A tiger stalked by a pool and a cheetah awoke on its delicately balanced perch.

The horse came, steadily galloping by the edge of the forest, brushing its mane against the low boughs of trees, when someone leapt on its back. Lava began riding the horse, first grabbing tufts of its mane. A whistle, and Kusa jumped from a low branch and ran alongside the horse as it galloped. He heaved himself up with the sheer exhilaration of the moment and sat astride it, behind Lava. They rode with freedom and happiness, never having known such power, communion or speed. At thirteen years of age they had dared to walk through the forest in the dark as they knew the language of their wild habitat and had befriended it. They rode the horse skirting the edge of the forest until they came close to the hermitage. They slowed the horse to a canter and then to a walk.

Valmiki had dozed off and his steady snoring whistled through the hermitage, circling it with a halo of restfulness. Sita awoke suddenly and dabbed the perspiration on her forehead with her sari. She had slept very peacefully and wondered why she had woken so abruptly. She heard Valmiki snoring, Urmilla muttering ingredients for a recipe in her sleep, then a soft thud. It was heavier than a fruit dropping at night, or the hoof of a goat. Then she heard the frenzied neigh of the horse.

From the moment the Ashwamedha horse disappeared under the shadow of the form that had leapt on its back, a code of whistles twittered between spies and messengers and relayed the information to the control tower at Ayodhya: *Ashwamedha captured; Rama challenged.*

Valmiki opened his eyes and wondered if what he was seeing now—the white Ashwamedha captured by Lava and Kusa—was a dream, or whether the seven boys he had seen so clearly taking flight as seven swans, when his eyes were closed in sleep, was a dream.

'Ma!' Lava grinned, enchanted. 'Look what was coming our way!' He led the horse to Sita as she stood up.

'There was no struggle, Ma, he came as if he belonged to us. He is ours now!' Kusa said, stroking the horse whose hot breath was cooling down. Its flesh quivered as Kusa smoothed the foaming sweat with his bare hands.

'This is such a beautiful creature, Ma. Please bless it as I want to gift it to you,' said Lava as he walked towards her.

Valmiki feared Sita was in shock. For both of them the first image that flashed in their minds, evoking a sense of defeat, was that the boys had not been schooled properly. The second image was a signal of fear as Sita saw her sons so radiant in their 'conquest' in this moment. She knew it would not last long. She could not say how, but her mother's intuition knew that Rama would not take this lightly.

'When . . . did this happen?' she found herself asking. The beauty of the boys, the horse, their sense of completeness and its ephemerality made her eyes swim. Valmiki saw her face from the corner of his eye. Sita gripped her right wrist with her left hand as it moved towards her pounding heart. Urmilla, who had crept beside her unnoticed, placed her hand on Sita's shoulder to steady her from falling into a spiral of self-doubt. Valmiki could sense the churning within Sita. Whatever she felt for Rama all those years ago and the way she had overcome the feeling of exile were now being turned upside down. Impulses of messages were flitting through her mind. 'Rama had never seen Lava; who was Kusa to him? After all, this was the Ashwamedha, and with his sense of duty, Rama would do everything that the ancestral rites and his people demanded of his authority.'

'Ma! We have not stolen anything. Why are you looking at us as if we have?' Lava had that look as he and Sita remembered the time he had picked out eggs from the sparrows' nest. She had to explain what the act of 'stealing' meant in the forest. 'Many things are here for us to eat, to take. But this nest is a home, and you are snatching away the bird's family; it's like fate stealing away our chances.' The words had stuck because he saw the pain in her eyes as she made him return the eggs to the nest.

'It was so natural . . . and it was running wild and free,' agreed Kusa, his teeth shining white as his smiling face caught the moonlight. He threw his head back in delight while gazing at the full height of the horse.

Valmiki did not want to interrupt any perspective or prism of the truth that was emerging; he was watching it unravel the way new leaves unfold in the warmth of the sun's rays. Urmilla knew that every strand of love, security, reasoning, confidence and responsibility in bringing up the boys was being tested. In the hermitage, in this forest, only Sita, Urmilla and Valmiki knew what the rules of society were, because they had lived in one. With the strange collision of their fates, they had brought the boys up in this wilderness with no assurances of what the future would bring. Sita had sent news of Lava's birth to Ayodhya, and it had been received with silence. The only way forward at that time seemed to have been to bring the boys up with no indication of their royalty, while enabling them to develop the presence of mind they needed to become masters of their future.

The horse's flesh twitched as it began shifting its weight from hoof to hoof. Both Lava and Kusa held on to its mane. Lava would not break his gaze in the direction of

Sita. Kusa whispered into the horse's ear as it dived its head down to shake its mane free. Each strand looked like a luminous moonbeam from where Sita, Valmiki and Urmilla stood. They could not ignore the sound of branches being brushed, twigs snapping, leaves squelching and the uneasy quiet of animals stalking as an unknown wave moved through the forest.

On hearing the news of the Ashwamedha's capture, Rama took on the challenge and rode out to the post that the messengers had signalled. He was accompanied by an entourage of his best soldiers, some on horseback and others on foot. Rama halted at the entrance to the hermitage, not knowing it was there. The tall branches formed an archway to the clearing, and the dazzling moonlight made only Lava, Kusa and the white horse visible.

'It would be wise to return that horse to its owner,' he said calmly. For Sita, Rama's voice still had that rumbling sweetness and calm authority that was never threatening, while its intention was not fully revealed to the listener.

'*We* found this horse, and he is ours now,' said the boys turning to him, unruffled.

'I can see that you found this horse, but this horse belongs to a ritual. You cannot stop its course. If you do, then the shastra says you must fight with me because I sent the horse out. It is clearly a mistake as you did not intend to harm anyone or indeed this beautiful creature.'

'Can you not see that this horse has now ended its journey and wants to be here?' said Lava, as Kusa cajoled the horse to eat grass out of his hand. The horse nuzzled comfortably against them.

'Ended its journey?' Rama smiled and his soldiers took a step further out from under the low branches. He raised his arm as a signal for them to step back. 'We all have rules by which our lives and the lives of others are kept in harmony. Otherwise we would be like the elements—constantly interrupted by the force of our energy which we cannot contain.'

'We are human,' Lava said with a degree of impatience.

'We too are made up of the elements,' Kusa added with his winning smile.

'But there is an order and a sequence in the elements—when water rises clouds are formed; in time the thunder rolls and the rain falls,' Rama continued, almost enchanted by the possibility of a discussion on cause and effect in the soft light.

'Why not speak plainly, even if you are on such a high horse!' said Lava. In spite of his stubborn hold on the Ashwamedha, Lava was engaged by this stranger who spoke to him in a voice that bathed everything in the cool moonlight.

'The horse belongs to my kingdom. It is part of a great sacrifice. You have stopped its course. That is a challenge.'

'We will fight for the horse.'

'You both are engaging in fantastical and unachievable claims and I do not wish to cause you harm. Besides, I can only fight an equal. Neither of you is close to me in age, and indeed, in the middle of the night, I cannot fight two wilful boys who have spent their lives in the forest.'

'Who do you think you are?' Lava said. Sita stood still in the dark without breathing. Rama could not have been aware of her, Valmiki or Urmilla sheltering in the cavernous shade of the tall trees.

'And who, may I ask, are you?' said Rama.

Lava began: 'I was born at the first stroke of that hour past midnight when darkness moves towards daylight. They said of my birth that Brahma visited and wrote his name on my forehead. I cannot take this as praise as I am a guest of those who brought me into the world, bloody, screaming and fighting on a full-moon night.

'My lessons stood for my father, and my teacher gave me a world where I could learn to read with my breath, my tongue, my eyes, my inner eye, my touch, taste and smell.

'My teacher's Teacher taught me
how to shape friendship from anger,
peace from haste,
going slow while travelling with speed,
learning silence from the dance of the trees
and singing with the insects to test an opinion.

'My closest companion is here, my brother, and his heartbeat and mine are one.

'We both were placed in the forest, our kingdom of reason where we learnt what is cruelty and what justice, and the language of beings that do not share our tongue.

'All this we could not have done without the one who filled my ears with the first story of how life came to be. So, listen to the story of my beginnings, as neither age nor status, kin or clan, can lay claim to true ancestry.

'My mother is spirit and earth. Her eyes shine like stars and when she left her girlhood she carried that light into her husband's home. My father, from her account, was a man who embodied compassion; and truth was the one jewel he wore when he lived a life of prosperity. When fortune's wayward winds began to blow, my father held on to truth as an anchor in the stormy sea of unimaginable events. My mother did not just witness his misfortune but decided to travel with him and give him courage. "After all," she often said, "what is the point of love if it cannot weather all seasons?"'

Rama had been listening as a patient bystander. His mind was open to listening—as a king he would hold an audience and listen to news and grievances before pronouncing his verdict or decreeing a law. He was enchanted by the musicality of the boy's voice. The poetry of Lava's language seemed unusual for a forest-dweller.

Rama was impressed by the boy's indignation at having to prove that the horse now belonged to him and his brother. It was evident they would challenge Rama. The boy seemed to have an interesting story but his ancestry would never be equal to the lineage of a king, so Rama was relieved on the boy's behalf that he need never fight him.

It was when he heard 'what was the point of love . . .' that something rippled through Rama. It seemed to echo words from a very deep yet unforgotten chamber in his heart. Rama decided to listen more intently to the boy and discover what was happening to him as the story unravelled.

'And what kind of misfortune was it that befell them?' Rama asked, in spite of himself.

'My father, she says, was a man who knew what was expected of him, and he followed the path of honour and truth. When the time came for him, soon after they were married, to take charge of the whole family, he was sent away with no reason except that his father wanted it so. As his father lay dying, unable to speak except through the words of another, my mother insisted she travel with my father to the lands where he was decreed to roam nameless. He did not wish her to suffer hardship but she would not be reasoned with, because, as she continues to say, "what is the point of love if it cannot weather all seasons?"

'Thirteen years they spent travelling across lands, meeting people who came to them with their stories. Wherever they went they were welcomed because they lived simply and found ways of easing the burden of other peoples' lives, in spite of having their own. One day, my mother, by yet another unfortunate storm of fate, was snatched away from their life as travellers to another country against her will. She was held captive and, against all odds, my father, with the help of his dearest friend and his brother, rescued my mother and overthrew the inglorious king who had oppressed his own people, and thus restored their peace.

'My father and mother returned to their family home and, following a warm welcome, my father took on the business of his people. I started growing within my mother. My father, kind, compassionate, heroic and honest as he was, delighted in the future. Again, by some unseen mischief, my mother was sent away, never to return to her home, her husband's heart, again.

'So great was her grief, greater than when she had been imprisoned in another land, that she could have ended her life . . .'

Rama knew this was beyond analogy or metaphor—it was his story. All his life he had seen beyond the immediate moment, always in preparation, always generous and conscious of what he owed others. It usually turned out to be the business of doing the right thing. Anyone who was a part of himself, like Sita, Lakshmana and Hanuman, was treated by him the way he treated himself—a sense of selfhood with a sense of self-abnegation. Sita had given him a sense of his self in the physical world and all that was in it.

Over the years, after he had banished her and Lakshmana had not returned, he was in a void of hearing counsel. The only body he knew was the state. But now, his life was told in a story by the boy, unmistakably his son.

Rama got down from his horse, so gently that neither of the boys felt it necessary to be on guard, and knelt close to Lava.

'But she knew,' Lava continued, 'that life is a chain of energy. Letting herself live and give birth to me were not merely endurance. She had ascended beyond the chains of name, birth, caste, clan—she is the one who gave me light.' Lava paused. Rama took the boy's right hand and placed it on his own head. All he could utter was 'Sita, Sita . . . Sita' with long-lost joy.

Valmiki and Urmilla were awed by Lava's rendering of his mother's life, with Kusa's accompaniment, from what he had gathered over the years. They were relieved that they would not have to intervene in any struggle to save the boys' lives. The boys had come of age.

They stretched out their arms to support Sita. The warm breeze made everything come to life. The leaves shivered and there was a stream of light where she stood. There was no pain or need for reconciliation. Sita had ascended time cycles. She turned to face the footfall that was behind her. 'All would be well for a while,' she thought and cried out, 'Hanuman!'

A Note

'[A] novella is often restricted to a single episode or event,
leading to an unexpected turning point [wendepunkt]'
Professor John Mullan[1]

Sita's Ascent is, in the form of a novella, a retelling of Sita's
story and a reimagining of the idea of woman as goddess.
Three things inspired me in this undertaking: the first was
the fascination with a literary form that would best tell a
woman's story—as when others tell us about something
that happened to someone we know. The second was the

---

[1] Cited in the *Guardian* Book Club by John Mullan, 'A Christmas
Carol' by Charles Dickens, discussing the form of the novella.
Accessed 16 December 2011.

inspiration that is Sita—an exiled queen, an expectant mother abandoned and left alone, undaunted by the extraordinary circumstances that are thrust upon her by the husband she continues to love. Thirdly, the function of memory as a metaphor for 're-membering' a dismembered story because it is told to us infrequently and in parts, and for experiencing culture through its epic characters.

I will start with the third point. Memory is a powerful tool that makes reflection possible by recalling through this process of rejoining with the past. A.K. Ramanujan's essay 'The Ring of Memory' demonstrates this with inimitable clarity while relooking at Kalidasa's *Sakuntala*.

King Dushyanta, after rejecting Sakuntala when she arrives at his court, regains his memory as a result of seeing the lost ring that eventually dispels the curse of the angry muni. Dushyanta's repentance facilitates a process of remembrance; a re-membering of dismembered memory. Sakuntala's absence is made present by his longing that is recounted in the poetry, not solely about her physical attributes but also the essence of her *being* that afforded him companionship in the alien world of the forest where he first met her, and as his soulmate.

Sakuntala's and King Dushyanta's longing and loss are metaphoric of exile. Memory is sharpened by longing. I experienced this exile in re-membering and retelling Ramayana in spaces and cultures that knew little or nothing of the epic's origin or sensibilities. Familiarizing myself with the characters *as real people* acted as a trigger of cultural memory. A retelling gives us new insights that could, and should be allowed to, make meaning of what is valued across cultures, in spite of different traditions.

Sita's Ascent for me began as a pause; a remembering of the epic with a new idea of who Sita is. Like many, I have often wondered what happens when a character goes beyond the realm of the author's imagination. I wanted to re-member Sita's essence through a reconstruction of events that were outside the familiar in the epic. In *Sita's Ascent*, I have endeavoured to enter into the future of someone from an epic tradition, who continues, through change, to haunt our imagination.

In performance storytelling, I have worked on the prequel—Rama's story. I have always been struck by a folk rendition of the episode when Rama is going into exile. He pleads with Sita not to come to the forest. To this she replies, 'Rama, in all versions of the Ramayana, Sita has gone to the forest. Without Sita, there *is* no Ramayana.'[2] Sita is central to the plot.

For me, it is this idea of Sita as a character who is

[2] Paula Richman, *Many Ramayanas: The Diversity of a Narrative Tradition in South Asia* (Berkeley: University of California Press, 1991).

conscious of her choices in spite of what happens to her, and the circumstances under which she is placed (by authors and storytellers), that is a trigger. This makes her empathetic, inventive and resourceful—she is able to ride out the terror that strikes her.

The second thing: Sita as inspiration. For me, the 'idea' of Sita is for all time. The idea enables a matrix so that when I place her across several time zones and continents, she ends up lighting the way even when she is violently abandoned.

In *Sita's Ascent*, the character challenges the author, as well as the reader, to follow a narrative through the remembrances of the people with whom she lived in the time of the epic. But this story is not merely about the perspectives of other people on Sita. I attempt to create a new story, a fiction, by drawing upon an age-old familiarity with the different characters in the epic.

Thus far, our popular imagination has been filled with a Ramayana story and its direct association with Deepavali or Diwali in some parts of India. The many representations of the epic that have originated in India assume that the story is solely Indian. I make a case and celebrate that this is not so. It is true that the third and fourth generation Indian diaspora across the world continue to keep the epic alive mostly with the story of Rama and Sita. Of special interest to me are the South East Asian versions that have the effect of sliding doors—dealing with the familiar in an unfamiliar way, affording greater depth to both character and action.

I have drawn on Sita and her situations from diverse sources. These helped me to see her as everywoman, epic hero and goddess.

My search for a multidimensional Sita began as an exploration for a character who goes beyond Valmiki. In doing so, Sita continues to be the familiar character we know, while she goes on to create a new plot line. In *Yuganta*, Iravati Karve had set the framework for first-person narratives. Here too the omniscient author is made redundant. The protagonist invites the reader to follow a narrative spoken in the voice of other characters that she has come in contact with. It is akin to an exchange of tales, possibly gossip, or, as attributed to the origin of storytellers and their tales, 'this is how the story came my way, and this is how I see it'.

The origin of a character is often seen to have little relevance to the unfolding of a story. I found that in many cultures parents tell their children about how they were born, what their strengths were. It would be interesting if a child were to reverse that process and inquire about the story of the mother. So, in the chapter 'Mandodari', I have combined narratives about Sita's origins and birth—or migrations of spirit and body—from an English translation of the Sanskrit *Adbhuta Ramayana* and from the Thai *Ramakian* in Garrett Kam's Ramayana in *The Arts of Asia*.

Lakshmana's end is influenced by the *Kirtivasa Ramayana* from Bengal. The laughter of Lakshmana, as a result of Nidra's visit, is inspired from an account in 'A Ramayana of Their Own: Women's Oral Narrative in Telugu' by Velcheru Narayana Rao in *Many Ramayanas*. Urmila's role as a midwife who describes Sita's labour here has been directly influenced by the traditional songs that sing of women, particularly Kausalya, giving birth.

While many Ramayanas have been researched and presented and published, my interest as a storyteller lay in being inspired by these sources that acted as a catalyst in writing the story of Sita, beyond Ramayana. The exploration of these sources shaped my direct experience of storytelling—identifying with a story and making meaning of the past by seeing it as a metaphor for the present.

As part of world literature, Sita's courage is indomitable and takes on epic dimensions in the emotional and geographical landscapes she traverses. We rarely see her in the safe interiors of palaces for very long; wilderness and abandon is where she triumphs.

This came to me while preparing Ramayana in two different stages and contexts. The first, Deepavali in India.

It was celebrated both at home and in whichever city, town or outpost my father's military posting had located us during the 1960s. Amamma, my maternal grandmother visited us during the season, and always took the trouble to bring the wooden dolls of Tirupathi, dressing them up for the Pattabhishekaham coronation, and stage the story of Rama and Sita. As an oral poet her compositions in Telugu were lyrical and her improvisations, theatrical. In her telling, Sita embodied the narrative of the canonized version, but her interpolations added a human dimension to Sita's character. Her Sita had the spirit of Agni, or fire, which was very liberating for Amamma as a storyteller and indeed for her generation. Sita's DNA of fire could be expressed in a myriad emotions that ranged from irritation to love, rage against injustice to fortitude and compassion. A range of emotions any sixteen-year-old young woman could relate to till she was thirty, in response to her life and the choices she made that created new challenges for her. It was this that made Sita awe-inspiring for me.

The second, 1988 in England. The Victoria and Albert Museum had an exhibition of Ramayana that was touring Cartwright Hall, Bradford. These were sixteenth-century Mughal miniatures. As a student who had just arrived from India to pursue a PhD at The Workshop Theatre, department of drama in the School of English, University of Leeds, I met the curator Dr Nima Smith with some enthusiasm. Over our shared interest in postcolonial literature, I was invited to give a lecture on the Hindu epic. I was with an English colleague from my department who then proceeded to ask, 'And, what is Ramayana?' It was an incredible moment like the Big Bang in my career of storytelling. Unknown to myself, I had a cultural gene that was from that moment propelled into a cross-fertilization of histories of ideas. Context was imperative for retelling.

The story of Rama and Sita and their adventures has always been a tale told and listened to in India. Having heard Ramayana from the age of three, I had never felt the need to categorize the ethnicity, culture, religion or nationality of the spaces and audiences when I heard it in different places. In fact, when I was leaving Madras for Leeds to study, Ramanand Sagar's *Ramayana*, the TV series, had set a world record in viewership. For the first time, everything came to a standstill—public transport, daily routines, visits—during the time the weekly thirty-five-minute episode was on. Hindus and non-Hindus were gripped by the dramatization and the epic brought India under its spell in its televised avatar.

I suddenly realized my entire context was different—Ramayana was a symbol; its characters functioned as points of reference in any professional, public or domestic situation while I was in India. Here, in Leeds, let alone

England, it was unknown, unloved, and discussed fairly
clinically among curators and scholars of archived South
Asian collections. As a reflex, I thought the best place to
start explaining to my colleague was to mention that the
epic was compelling as it had possibly inspired some of
the characters for George Lucas's *Star Wars* (1977).[3] It
was sheer postcolonial reflex to bridge cultural gulfs with
cinema, and that too, with Hollywood.

[3] Writing about *The Jedi in the Lotus* by Steven Rosen (Arktos:
London, 2010), Charles S.J. White says:

Rosen's study shows the influence of *Star Wars* on Joseph
Campbell, Mircea Eliade and other major scholars of
mythology who were consulted by Lucas to develop his
understanding. These scholars were steeped in the lore
of the hero in the Mahabharata and Ramayana, as well
as other aspects of the Indian tradition. Their theories
impacted 'the creator of Star Wars,' who said, 'I'm telling
an old myth in a new way.'

A striking outcome of Rosen's analysis is possibly to
heighten the interest of readers in the relevance of the
mythic traditions of India to the sensibility of a modern
cinematic artist. With that deeper insight they are given
the opportunity through George Lucas's films to journey
imaginatively to participate with him in the reality of
India's ancient mythic experience. (Quoted from *The Jedi
in the Lotus* Facebook fan page)

I did a twenty-minute overview of the popular version of the Ramayana to explain why there were Mughal miniatures from the ateliers of Persian schools about a Hindu epic, collated by English collectors—I had crossed the desert of my mind in assuming that Ramayana was owned exclusively by India; India was only its birthplace. The migration of the story, the cross-fertilization of versions, the myriad manifestations through oral and written literature, the forms of dissemination in performing and visual arts and crafts had indeed made it a world story. The linearity of the story and those who had reinvented it in their writings through the ages had made it the first novel in world literature. When I finished, my colleague said, 'Instead of the lecture, why not *tell* the story?' And that's just what I did, with the miniatures functioning as a traditional scroll.

On my arrival in Leeds, writer and essayist Caryl Phillips had suggested a writing exercise—to think of all the things that struck me as new and different before I got used to them. It could have been public transport, escalators, dialects of English. The question 'What is Ramayana?' had that effect on me, of seeing the familiar from an unfamiliar viewpoint. This was the epic that had been seasoned by Amamma's recitals, that had inspired the Indian independence movement, that boosted the economy during Hindu festivals, that was embedded in political and social contexts and one that had kept the oral tradition of performance alive throughout the world.

In an age when England was becoming serious about addressing its multiculturalism—schools in Bradford, Birmingham and Leicester, besides the boroughs in London, had 40 per cent black and Asian students in classrooms—my Ramayana was leading the way across curriculums in primary and secondary schools, and as performance in venues for art and in concert halls, with the greeting of 'Diwali Mubarak'. I was learning at each telling how to interpolate contemporary references from British news within the story; in turn, audiences related to the contexts within an Indian epic that was fundamentally about the human struggle to live by certain ideals. Story or epic, the Ramayana became a window to a cultural sensibility or to an Indian way of thinking.

❧

And, finally, the first thing: my fascination for exploring a literary form to tell a woman's story.

What is at the heart of *Sita's Ascent*? It is an exploration of the psychological dimension that reveals Sita's human condition. It allows identification and empathy with Sita, instead of viewing her as a victim. Had Sita been a victim she would not have survived.

A Note

In 1998, Kathleen Hamilton, CEO of Leicester Haymarket Theatre Trust commissioned me to write and perform Ramayana, in a city with 30 per cent Asians of Indian, Pakistani and East African origin and predominantly Gujarati speakers. This was directed by Chris Banfield (who was at the time the deputy head of the department of theatre studies at the University of Birmingham, having directed the works of Girish Karnad and Badal Sircar and those of other contemporary Indian dramatists). He integrated the music of internationally renowned percussionist Colin Seddon. The storytelling performance was now two hours long and had a simple but evocative set and lighting design by Jenny Campbell.

In the years before, the episodic action of Rama and Sita's life had been the driving force behind my performances. For the first time, working with a theatre director made it possible for me to chart the many narratives from Paula Richman's work as well as use my own encounters with the regional versions. I wanted to adapt these for a staged, dramatic version for viewers who were both familiar and unfamiliar with the cultural contexts, that is, East African Asians and British audiences.

This was when I first started focusing on the psychological aspects of the characters in Ramayana, which led them to their actions. My interest was caught by the thread of Sita's story, in spite of her absence in Ramayana till she makes her decision to accompany Rama into exile. Yes, she is crucial to the plot and structure of the epic. But a remembrance of her, a search for her and her absence make her essential qualities come alive.

In Ramayana, it is the women who propel the action—Ahalya, Manthara, Kaikeyi, Soorpanakka and Sita. And the stories backstage, the hidden women—Urmilla, Mandodari—began to gain a voice that told me more about Sita. But live performances never allow for that kind of time and space, not with theatre time directives. What the performance and dramatization did allow was to get the characters to exchange dialogue, revealing their relationships, longings, struggles, joys and their empathy with the human condition, even though they were worshipped as gods in another culture. Among the different Indian philosophies and systems of thinking, being and becoming, there is one that talks about unlocking the divine in the human. Here was an opportunity to discover what it meant to be human, in all its colours of despair, love beyond abandonment, rage and compassion. Most empathetic parents want to leave behind a story for their children. I doubt they do it out of the need to achieve immortality as much as out of their unconditional love which they feel should remain a constant thread for their children despite the changes in the world. That, for me, is Sita's ascent—the heaviness of what she endures illumines and embraces the human condition with triumph. It is not about victory, conquest or martyrdom; it is about resourcing a daily energy to overcome with lightness and love.

In one sense, Sita is an inheritance and a legacy for many women, not an imposition. While reimagining Sita and her story, it was an enriching journey to enter into the idea that Sita is exiled and adopted—both literally and metaphorically—by the country endorsed as 'marriage'. In our times, endurance in women is precariously interpreted as the attribute of a 'victim', but Sita has resourcefulness, fortitude, cheerfulness and an ocean of love despite being placed in circumstances not of her choosing, as an orphan and an exile.

Tithiksha, or forbearance, affords the simultaneous ability to experience the immediate without losing sight of what endures against all odds. Sita here radiates across time, challenging every author to write the story she directs. She is never dour or tragic, and she is increasingly spontaneous and defiantly compassionate.

～

Sita's Ascent is a storyteller's imagining of a character from an epic that has been told and retold over millennia. From the familiar it plunges into the labyrinth of the unfamiliar, casting a new light on a quality that goes out of fashion because of its 'moral' overtones in the past. This retelling is about getting into the fibre, life and essence of a person who is an icon.

As a storyteller I could opt for a path of recitation and/ or interpolation. Both keep the folk and oral epic traditions alive. But it is the interpolators who have made their stories evolve across politics, resistances and history by placing the familiar characters in challenging circumstances, within the context of contemporary occurrences, to renew their endurance.

In *Sita's Ascent* the real storyteller is Hanuman who remains silent, watches the drama and takes action. He is able to enter Sita's inner world and witness her ability to engage with the urgent and the immediate, while she simultaneously understands and expresses the call of what is constant in life.

So much in life happens due to miscommunication, thoughts felt and left unexpressed, roles that have to be played—even when there is love. Because there is love, the greater is the pain of endurance when there is loss or absence, which offers us a spiral of reflection. Only the truly buoyant can weather it and come out of it radiant. Hanuman, in this novella, signals that for us—Sita's ascent is more powerful because we see it coming.

Acknowledgements

It was a privilege when Kamini Mahadevan invited me to embark on the Sita story. Thanks to her and Penguin and the many readers who have seen it through. I thank Chris Banfield as a director for an inspirational process in keeping the epic alive across cultures, Lakshmi Holmström for her continued reading and observations; placing 'The Ring of Memory', among other essays, and her evocative translations from Ramayana in my path; and introducing me to Paula Richman, to whom I am indebted for her incredible research and generosity. Dr David Schulman, Dr Stuart Blackburn, Dr Velacheru Narayana Rao and Richard Blurton for endorsing my 'English' retelling of Ramayana. Dr Darryll Grantley, Dr Nicola Shaughnessy, Emily Parrish, Dan Thompson, Craig Jenkins and all my students from the University of Kent for participating in it; Ben Haggarty for festivalizing it; Di Cooper for using it in a session in Central School of Speech and Drama; Colin Seddon for his mammoth undertaking with the music; and Kathleen Hamilton with Leicester Theatre Trust, Kulbir Natt and the Barbican who created platforms for it across twenty-two years, which are still running. Dr Mukulika Banerjee, Judy McKnight, Dee Ashworth, Raji Krishnan, as trustees of the Vayu Naidu Storytelling Theatre Company, for championing it, the Arts and Humanities Research Council with the University of Kent, Canterbury, and Arts Council England for funding the research, development and founding of this platform of work.

Last but not least, to my grandmother, Allarmelu Mangathai Calpakkam Karunanidhi Naidu, and my beloved mother, Jayarukmini Naidu, and father, Major General Aban Naidu, who are remembered as the great storytellers straddling cultures to keep the epic alive. Hari Sagar Naidu for his ocean of compassion, Upendra Sagar for his idealism and Viji Vasudev for her Ramayana for children. To my cousin Urmilla, who taught me the meaning of her name, and to Krishna for the note and your attentive reading.

Swami Tripurananda is thanked for his discussions on Tithiksha and its relevance. Usha Aroor for being an early and constant guide in the complexities of epics and their characters and for placing *Yuganta* in my hands thirty years ago.

To Chris, my husband of many lives, this is a simple dedication thanking you for your epic endurance and hospitality to all the characters in this novella who stayed for as long as they wanted in our home; to Unmai who always understands when it is time for silence and rest, and for alerting me to the compassion hidden in the strength of Hanuman.

This work is for Thakur, with love, who is there when it all happens. And now, over to Sita.

YOU MAY ALSO LIKE

Lost Loves: Exploring Rama's Anguish
Arshia Sattar

'[A] profound and wise book . . . Sattar shows us how
the complexity of [Sita's] character in Valmiki affects
Rama's morally questionable actions . . . [She] makes
us realise how deeply conflicted Rama is'—Wendy
Doniger in *Outlook*

The story of the Ramayana is a story of trial and tribulation, of the
subtlety of right and wrong, of love and loss. The actions of Rama
have perplexed readers over millennia. *Lost Loves* is an attempt to
come to terms with Rama and with the Ramayana.

The essays in this book imagine what Rama and Sita might
have thought and felt in those terrible years of exile. They explore
what happens to love in separation, and how public lives and
private desires collide to devastating effect. Arshia Sattar makes
the existential conflicts of the Ramayana fascinatingly relevant and
freshly inspiring for the contemporary reader.

'[Sattar] is one of the finest interpreters of our time . . . She
[lays] bare the nuanced dilemmas [in the Ramayana]'—*Mint*

'The reader will be stunned by the questions Sattar raises'
—*Business Standard*

Non-fiction
Rs 250

In Search of Sita
Edited by Malashri Lal and Namita Gokhale

'The essays and conversations [in this book] direct us not only to their content, but to our own questions about Sita'—Urvashi Butalia in *Mail Today*

Sita is one of the defining figures of Indian womanhood, yet there is no single version of her story. Canonical texts deify Sita while regional variations humanize her. Sacrifice, self-denial and unquestioning loyalty are some of the ideals associated with Sita. But the Janaki who symbolized strength, who could lift Shiva's mighty bow and who courageously chose to accompany Rama into exile, is often forgotten.

In Search of Sita presents essays, conversations and commentaries that explore different aspects of her life. It revisits mythology, reopening the debate on her birth and her different trials, offering fresh interpretations of this enigmatic figure and her indelible impact on our everyday lives.

'The wide net cast by the editors captures several creative and critical shades in limning Sita'—*The Hindu*

'This book is a nuanced effort to explode the myth of the unidimensional Sita'—*Delhi Midday*

Anthology
Rs 399